Judge McBain shook his head. "Boyd must have known his other plans wouldn't work out. His gunslinger didn't scare you into letting his son go—so now Boyd's going to raze the town. That's the only thing left." He squinted up at the clock. "Nine hours before that train gets here. I wonder if we're going to make it."

Matt Ramsey wished he could have given the judge a positive answer. But with twenty gunnies waiting on the edge of town, the odds had shifted in favor of Boyd, especially since nobody in town seemed willing to fight him.

Now Ramsey himself glanced up at the clock.

Nine hours.

Ramsey had to wonder how many of them would still be alive by the time the train rolled into town. . . .

Also in THE RAMSEYS series

**THE RAMSEYS
RAMSEY'S LUCK
MATT RAMSEY
BLOOD MONEY
RAMSEY'S GOLD
DEATH TRAIL
RAMSEY'S BADGE
THE DEADLY STRANGER
COMANCHE
BAD BLOOD
DEATH HUNT**

GUNDOWN
WILL McLENNAN

JOVE BOOKS, NEW YORK

GUNDOWN

A Jove Book / published by arrangement with
the author

PRINTING HISTORY
Jove edition / May 1991

All rights reserved.
Copyright © 1991 by Jove Publications, Inc.
This book may not be reproduced in whole or in part,
by mimeograph or any other means, without permission.
For information address: The Berkley Publishing Group,
200 Madison Avenue, New York, New York 10016.

ISBN: 0-515-10569-4

Jove Books are published by The Berkley Publishing Group,
200 Madison Avenue, New York, New York 10016.
The name "JOVE" and the "J" logo
are trademarks belonging to Jove Publications, Inc.

PRINTED IN THE UNITED STATES OF AMERICA

10 9 8 7 6 5 4 3 2 1

GUNDOWN

CHAPTER ★1★

1

A drunk was the first person to see the five men ride into town.

Even in his condition, the drunk could tell there was something odd about the riders. Maybe it was the hard way they looked around the town, not as if they were trying to see what pleasures it might yield but were instead trying to find out where a man with a rifle might hide or a gunman might duck for cover. Also there was the fact that each rider wore not only a .44 and a holster but also had a long Winchester filling his scabbard.

The five riders ended up at the livery stable. The limping black man who was the livery owner's assistant came out and greeted them. The men started laughing and poking each other and trading jokes. Even from here the drunk could tell they were making fun of the colored man.

The five men then walked up the center of the dusty street. At 6:45 A.M. the day's traffic was just now rumbling into the streets, horses and buckboards and wagons. The men kept glancing around, and again the drunk had the impression that they were searching out places where they might hide later on.

Center Street, the town's main drag, was five blocks of false fronts, though Center could claim two genuine red brick buildings with more to come within six months or so. Congreve, the town itself, served farmers and miners within a one-hundred-mile radius. Now that the boom had moved on farther west—you heard a lot of rumors about a silver strike in Colorado—things were more peaceful and civilized in Congreve. Gold sometimes made men, even good men, crazy and violent.

The drunk looked up as the men walked toward him. He cringed at the thought of what they might do to him.

He started to grab hold of one of the supports holding up the roof, but a rough hand pushed him back down.

A man with a week's growth of beard and a pink knife scar slanting down his right cheek laughed and said, "You stay right where you are, old-timer. I don't want to have a drink in any place that would serve you."

"Where the hell's the jail in this burg, anyway?" said another man. He was the only one of the five to wear a business suit. It was dark, with wide lapels, and too heavy for early September weather. He had a gold front tooth and perhaps the meanest dark eyes the drunk had ever seen.

The drunk said, "Two blocks down. One block over."

The man in the suit paid the drunk no form of thanks or recognition. He just pushed past him, slamming him against the support as he did so.

Once the men had passed through the batwing doors, the drunk decided to gain a little favor with the man who was always arresting him for public intoxication, Sheriff Sam Curry.

Why would five of the roughest-looking men the drunk had ever seen ride into town early in the morning and ask where the jail was?

Only one reason the drunk could think of: they were men sent by George Boyd to get his son John out of jail, where he had been sitting the past two days charged with the murder of a town girl he'd been seeing.

Everybody had been talking about what George Boyd would do. As the richest and most powerful rancher in this part of the state, he was pretty much a law unto himself. It didn't hurt that he was best friends with two of the state federal judges. But this time judges weren't going to be of much help to him. Right after being found in a barn where he was sleeping off a drunk, John Boyd had confessed his guilt to Sheriff Curry.

The drunk hurried through the long shadows of the dawn streets.

Sheriff Curry had better know about these men. And fast.

2

The attack had come sometime during the night. Curry had gotten up from bed to get a drink of water, and suddenly the pain had started like fire up his right arm and then spread over across his chest.

It was then he'd called out for his daughter, Rita. She'd come running, of course. Rita always did. Her father's health had been her primary concern since the death of her mother eight years earlier.

Rita had recognized immediately what was wrong. Her

father was having another heart attack. He'd had five of them over the past ten years, the third one almost proving fatal.

Once she'd gotten him resting comfortably in bed, she'd flown out the door, searching desperately for two people—Doc Gaines and her father's friend who was staying at the hotel for the night, Matt Ramsey.

After spending two hours at Curry's tidy little house, Matt Ramsey had walked back to the hotel and gotten as much sleep as he could. He'd always found sleeping during daylight hours impossible. He dozed only an hour or so before dawn brought squawking birds and strutting roosters and the noise of a small town coming alive.

There was another reason he couldn't sleep. Sheriff Curry, his old friend from Civil War days, had asked Matt to take over his job until ten-thirty tonight, at which time the train would arrive and the prisoner John Boyd would be put aboard to face justice in the state capital. Curry felt his deputy was too young and raw for such responsibility. He said he hated to ask Matt, but given Curry's condition, he didn't have much choice.

Matt could hardly say no to an old friend who might be dying.

So he'd gone back to his hotel room and slept a troubled hour. At some point he dreamt of his family, of his brother Amos and Amos's wife Rose Margaret and their children back on the family farm in Fannin County; of Luke, second youngest at twenty, who'd just wed a Jack County girl, the both of them running horses on a small place up on the Trinity; and of brother Kyle still searching for gold in Colorado. Even though they kept in touch, the war had scattered them and changed them—hell, the despair and poverty that followed the war had helped kill their mother, father and sister. And now the Ramseys, like too many Americans, wandered and roamed the land. . . .

He got up, went down the hall, washed up and shaved, went back to his room and put on clean clothes. Then he strapped on his gun belt.

Finally, his boots on, he took the sheriff's badge that Curry had given him and pinned it on his blue shirt.

Glancing at himself in the mirror, he saw how quickly and certainly wearing a badge changed a man. You didn't look at his face. You just looked at his badge. And all that it represented. That's why every gunny in the West couldn't wait to bag himself a lawman. Because any man who wore the six-pointed star had to be a very special catch.

Matt touched the pearl handle of his revolver and left the room a lean, dark-haired sheriff with smiling brown eyes that hinted faintly of some vague sorrow.

The good smell of morning coffee greeted Ramsey as he walked into the sheriff's office.

Dennis Quinn, the deputy, was just pouring himself a cup. As soon as he saw Ramsey, he started a second cup going.

The office was small and tidy. Two small desks faced each other, one for the sheriff, one for the deputy. On one wall was a small glass-and-wood bookcase filled with impressive-looking legal tomes. On the other wall were two gun racks, each filled with carbines and shotguns. A heavy wooden door led to the cells in back. Along with the coffee, the office smelled of cigarette smoke. Paper and a pack of Bull Durham lay on the deputy's desk.

Quinn, a short young man with the beginnings of a paunch and too many worry lines for a twenty-five-year-old man, handed Ramsey the steaming tin coffee cup and said, "Heard from Rita. About her dad and all. And you bein' acting sheriff."

Ramsey smiled. "I don't plan to give you any orders."

"Fine with me if you did." Quinn nodded his prematurely graying head to the door leading to the cells. "I just spelled the night deputy. He said everything went fine last night." Quinn's mouth tightened anxiously. "That means it's still ahead of us."

"Ahead of us?"

"Yeah. What the kid's old man is going to do."

Ramsey repressed a smile. Quinn couldn't be much older than the Boyd "kid." "Any ideas what that might be?"

"Nothin' specific. But I know George Boyd well enough to know that there's no way he's going to let his son be taken to the state capital to be tried for murder."

"I thought the son confessed."

"He did. But that won't stop his old man."

Ramsey sat on the edge of the desk and sipped his coffee. "It do me any good to ride out and see the father?"

Quinn shook his head. "Arrogant son of a bitch. Owns the mayor and owns the county attorney and even owns the Presbyterian minister. Plus he owns about half the good grazing land in this state."

Ramsey laughed. "Maybe I'd be a little arrogant, too."

"Might be funny to you, Ramsey, but you didn't grow up around here. I saw what the Boyds can do to a man. They did it to my pa. He owned a small general store. Boyd was his best customer. And he never let Pa forget it. Any time of night or day Boyd wanted something, Pa had to take care of him. Boyd knows how to make a man crawl."

"The son any different?"

Quinn shrugged. "Son's crazy. Real bad temper. Always

been that way. The old man never could control him."

"How come he confessed?"

Quinn snorted. "I know what you're thinking. He could've just sat tight and waited for his daddy to come and get him. But killing the girl—well, you'll see when you talk to him."

And it was then that the front door was slammed open and a drunken middle-aged man with about the saddest face Ramsey had ever seen staggered in. He wore a simple blue work shirt and loose-fitting cotton trousers. Both were filthy. He hadn't shaved for at least a week, and even from the threshold he stank enough that Ramsey's stomach tightened. Then there was the face, a hooked nose that had been broken several times, a mouth that trembled slightly even in repose and a pair of brown eyes a beagle would envy.

"Morning, Jim," Quinn said. "You here to sleep it off?" Quinn looked at Ramsey. "We've seldom got a full house, so Jim here generally comes in and sleeps all day." He spoke about the man as if he weren't there. "Used to be a fine, proud citizen. Then his wife got herself killed in a fire and he hasn't been worth a shit since. Right, Jim?"

Jim nodded mournfully then gathered himself and said, "Where's the sheriff?"

"Afraid he's sick," Ramsey said. "Something we can do for you?"

"Just wanted to tell you," Jim said, gulping and catching his breath.

"Tell us what?"

"About the men."

"What men?"

"Boyd's men. Least I'll bet they are." Jim wasn't one of those drunks who slurred his words. You could only tell how drunk he was by looking at his eyes, the horror and fatigue in them. That, and the way he weaved like a statue about to fall off its pedestal.

"How many of them, Jim?" Quinn said.

"Five."

"When they get in?"

"Little bit ago."

"At Barney's?"

"Yup."

"You sure they're Boyd's men?"

"Who else'd they be with the kid in jail?" Jim said.

Quinn set down his coffee. He sloped his flat-brimmed hat and touched the handle of his Navy Colt as if for luck. "Maybe I'd better get on over there and see what's up."

Ramsey set down his coffee cup, too. "Thanks for giving us the word, Jim."

"You be sure and tell the sheriff who told you?"

"I won't forget," Ramsey said. "I promise." He nodded to the door. "Now why don't you go on out of here and we'll take care of things."

Jim looked first at Ramsey then at the deputy. "You make sure he tells the sheriff, deputy?"

"I'll make sure."

"I want him to know I'm his friend."

"I'm sure he knows that," Ramsey said. "See you later, Jim."

Finally, Jim went out.

As the door was closing, Ramsey said, "And here I thought I was going to have an easy day. Just sit around and wait for the train to come in."

"You don't have to go, Matt. I'll do it."

Ramsey touched the finger where a wedding ring would go. "Can't help but notice you're wearing a ring."

GUNDOWN

The deputy glanced at his hand. "That I am. And I've got me a good wife."

"Kids?"

"Four."

"Think I'll take this one."

"Just because I'm married?"

Ramsey went over to the gun rack and took down a carbine. "Be a lot more people missing you than'd be missing me."

"You sure you want to do this, Matt?"

Ramsey hefted the carbine. "Got to do something to kill time in this town, don't I?" Then he quit kidding. "If I'm not back here in twenty minutes, maybe you'd better come over."

Deputy Quinn nodded and then gave a little salute of good-bye.

3

After the war, Harry Robson had taken up with a Confederate colonel who styled himself after the infamous Quantrill. They'd razed small towns, robbed banks, burned out settlers on the expanding frontier and even gone after certain small bands of Indians. He had been looking for a purpose in his life. The war had given him such a purpose. He had fought to preserve the Confederacy. But after the war . . . One day, Robson had caught the colonel cheating him on the split of a bank take and done the only fitting thing: he'd shot the man right in the face. Robson had then taken control of the small group of men, and ever since, they'd followed him. The problem was that with the appearance of such groups as the Pinkertons, and improved law enforcement throughout the West, the old type of lawlessness was pretty much over. So Harry Robson and his men had gradually become hired guns. Whenever rich or powerful men needed a certain type of job done, there was Robson and his ex-soldiers.

That's why they were in Congreve now. George Boyd's son was in jail here and about to be taken away for trial. This was where a man like Robson was useful.

As he stood at the bar, smoking and trying not to pay attention to the giggly way the other four men were carrying on with a very old and very tired whore, Robson touched the envelope of money in his black suit coat. George Boyd's first offer was money. Violence, if and when necessary, came later.

He pushed his shot glass back to the bartender for some more rye.

As he did so, he noticed that his men had stopped laughing.

Robson glanced up into the mirror behind the bar. Framed between the batwing doors was a tall, sinewy man packing a rifle and wearing a six-pointed star. He came into the saloon, his spurs loud against the sudden silence.

The lawman looked around the place and immediately decided who was in charge. He came over to Robson.

"Morning," he said.

"Morning, Sheriff."

"Wondered if we could have a little talk."

"Sure."

The lawman nodded to a poker table near the back of the place. "How about there?"

"Fine with me." Robson picked up his glass. "Care for a little refreshment?"

"Little early for me."

Robson smiled. "You must be a church-going man."

"Don't know that anybody'd accuse me of that exactly," the lawman said.

Robson noted that the sheriff let him lead the way to the table. The lawman walked at an angle. He didn't want the three men behind him to try anything stupid.

The lawman took the chair that put his back to the wall so nobody could come up from behind. This also gave him a clear look at Robson's four men.

The lawman said, "I'm Matt Ramsey."

He put out a gloved hand. The men shook.

"I guessed you weren't Sam Curry," Robson said.

"Sam's laid up. Heart attack."

Robson whistled. "Heart attack? That can be bad shit. That's how my own father went." He took a sip of whiskey. "So you're in charge, huh?"

Ramsey's gaze hardened. "Until tonight. Until I put John Boyd on the train."

Robson smiled. "I guess you know who sent us here, then."

"I guess I do."

"We didn't come to make any trouble."

"That makes me feel a whole lot better."

"You can be sarcastic if you want, Ramsey. But it's the truth."

Robson took the white envelope from his suit coat pocket and laid it on the table. "Know what's in there?"

"Guess I don't."

"Four thousand dollars. Yankee cash."

"Lot of money."

"And guess who it's for?"

"Who?"

"You. Since you're in charge, I mean."

"So it was intended for Sheriff Curry?"

"Yup."

"He'd never take it."

"Four thousand dollars in Yankee cash is a lot of money."

"You don't know Sam very well."

Robson looked him over. Ramsey struck him as hard, smart and shrewd. But he noticed how Ramsey's eyes kept dropping to the envelope. No man could resist the pull of that kind of money. "Maybe I don't know Sam Curry very well, Ramsey, but maybe I know you better than you think."

"Meaning?"

"Meaning you could have yourself a nice life on four thousand dollars. Maybe buy a little spread somewhere, get yourself a wife, start a family." Robson paused. "You were in the war, weren't you?"

"Yes."

"And I bet I know which side."

"Oh?"

"Same side I was on. The right side."

"Maybe."

"And ever since the war, Ramsey, you've been like me. Drifting. Looking for something. Not even sure what it is. But you keep looking. Only trouble is—" Here Robson smiled and pointed to his head, to the gray flecks that shot through his otherwise black hair. "Only trouble is, we're running out of time. We've got to throw in somewhere, with somebody, and get ready for our old age."

Robson pushed the envelope across the table to Ramsey. "I have to tell you how many head of cattle that would buy? How much grazing land?"

Ramsey looked at the money again then raised his eyes to Robson. "He confessed."

"A man gets drunk, he'll confess to practically anything. I don't take drunk talk seriously."

"He was sober when he confessed."

"You know what a jury's going to do to a young man named Boyd?" Robson said. "This'll be their way of paying back his father. The kid won't get a fair trial. All that jury'll care about is how fast they can hang him."

Robson touched the envelope again. "But why get ourselves all riled up here, Ramsey? Why don't we talk about something pleasant again?"

"Like four thousand dollars in Yankee cash?"

Robson smiled. "Exactly what I had in mind, Ramsey."

Ramsey shoved the money back to him. "Afraid I can't do it."

Robson shook his head then tipped his glass to the four men at the bar. "They're hoping you'll turn the money down."

"Oh?"

"If you were to take the money, they wouldn't have anything to do. They'd just saddle up a horse for John Boyd and then take him back to his father's ranch. And they wouldn't have any fun at all."

"I see."

"But if you turn the money down—" Robson shook his head again with dramatic sadness. He raised his eyes to Ramsey. "But if you turn the money down, then they'll have to fight to get Boyd out of jail. And they love to fight. It's all they've ever known. Hell, those boys were fourteen years old when they started fighting for the Confederacy. Fighting's their only pleasure." Just then the whore giggled. Robson made a face. "Except for ugly women, that is."

"You're telling me there's going to be a fight?"

"A bad one, I'm afraid."

"Even though he's confessed to killing her?"

"His father doesn't much care about that, Ramsey. He just wants his son back."

Ramsey looked over at the four men at the bar. "Then I guess there's going to be a fight."

Robson shook his head again. "These men know every dirty trick there is. And they're ruthless. Completely and totally ruthless. The kind of men Quantrill admired, if you understand what I mean. You really think the townspeople are going to back you up against men like these?"

"It's their town. They should."

"Sometimes people fool you, Ramsey. You give more credit for bravery than they deserve. During the war, I saw a lot of cowardice—men who'd rather you kill their wives than kill them; wives letting you have them to save their lives. When you come right down to it, Ramsey, most people don't have much respect for themselves."

Ramsey stood up. "If you change your mind, I'll be at the sheriff's office."

Robson smiled. "I guess we'll be seeing each other there, anyway. Now that you've made things inevitable."

"You could always go back to George Boyd and tell him you've decided to let the law take its course."

Robson laughed a whiskey laugh. "I could now, couldn't I, Ramsey? But what kind of self-respecting outlaw would do a thing like that? Because that's what I am, Ramsey. I learned that in the war. The only thing that gives me any meaning is fighting. In that sense, I'm like my men over there. Fighting is about the only thing that keeps me going."

Ramsey picked up the carbine he'd had leaning against his chair. "You're an intelligent man, Robson. Why don't you use your brains?"

And with that, Ramsey walked back toward the batwing

doors, moving again at an angle so he could keep an eye on the four men who were watching him with such eager interest.

One of the men, the one with a week's growth of black beard and a vicious scar down his cheek, pointed at Ramsey and said, "It's gonna be fun to kill you, Sheriff. It's going to give me pure pleasure."

Then they all laughed, including the whore, and Ramsey backed his way through the batwing doors.

CHAPTER
★2★

"He won't eat," Deputy Dennis Quinn said.

"Since when?" Ramsey said.

"Day before yesterday."

"He sick?"

"Not that I can tell."

"You bring him three meals a day?"

"We sure do."

"And he turns every one down?"

"Right."

Ramsey, leaning on the edge of the sheriff's desk, rubbed his jaw and looked at the rapidly cooling breakfast sitting on the desk opposite. Two poached eggs, three thick slices of bacon, two pieces of coarse wheat bread covered with honey, and fried potatoes all served on a nice little tray from the café down the street. Who could turn down a meal like that?

GUNDOWN

"Maybe it's time I go meet Mr. Boyd," Ramsey said.

Dennis Quinn shook his head. "Good luck."

Ramsey had just started for the cell door when the front door opened. In a long beam of dusty sunlight stood a fine-looking elderly gentleman dressed in an expensive gray suit and carrying a shiny black walking stick. He had the features of a Roman senator, complete with hawk nose and curly white hair. If he announced that he was running for the Presidency, Ramsey would probably vote for him on appearance alone.

"Morning, Mr. Stufflebeam."

"Morning, son," the elderly man said with only a hint of arrogance. He nodded to Ramsey. "And this must be the legendary Mr. Ramsey."

He crossed the office and put out his hand. Ramsey took it and they shook.

Quinn eyed the door. "Guess I'll mosey down the street. Make my usual morning stops."

Ramsey nodded goodbye. He wasn't sure exactly who this Stufflebeam was, but he had a pretty good idea why he was here.

"Like a cup of coffee, Mr. Stufflebeam?" Ramsey said.

"Rather have a stogie," Stufflebeam said, patting his chest with a broad, liver-spotted hand.

"Be my guest," Ramsey said.

Edwin Stufflebeam lighted his stogie and proceeded to tell Ramsey why he was here.

Behind the cell-block door, all the cells stood empty except the last one. On its thin cot lay a short, angular young man who needed both a shave and a bath. He wore a once-white shirt and expensive cord trousers, now dirty. Deep-set blue eyes gazed mournfully out of the face, looking at the small rectangle of sky seen through the bars high on the west-facing wall.

Every so often he'd see a bird arc against the sky, or a puffy white cloud push by, or a kid's kite flutter on the air currents, and he'd always think the same thing: that he wished he were a bird or a cloud or a kite.

He had the terrible feeling that this time he'd done something not even his father's money and power could get him out of. He had the terrible feeling that this time he was beyond the help of anybody. All he could think of was state prison and the images he'd heard of it over the years— the filthy cells, the strong, lusty men who'd gotten used to young men like himself as sex partners, and the violence, the seemingly perpetual violence of the place. It was estimated that twenty percent of the men there would be seriously wounded or murdered before they had served all their time. Lying in his cell here, he was already having nightmares about the place, the dank-smelling stone walls, the red-eyed rats chittering in the shadows, and the stomach-turning food that was served meal after meal.

He sat up on the edge of his cot now and started rubbing the back of his neck.

He wanted a bath and a shave and clean clothes and a good, fast horse.

He wanted to ride up to the bluffs where the long grasses smelled sweet on the breeze and the powerful golden sunlight cured whatever ailed you.

He wanted to float a raft down the rushing river again, to listen to his father's ranch hands tell ghost stories around the campfire.

He didn't want to be twenty-three years old. He didn't want to be charged with the murder of his former girlfriend, Amanda Sayles.

He wanted to be a kid again.

He wanted to be free.

He kept rubbing the back of his neck. He kept trying not to think of Amanda. Of what she'd said . . . about wanting to be done with him . . . of how she'd looked there in the grass, dead . . .

Then he'd started running, running, finally holing up in a sod-hut tavern five miles out of town; drinking until he was sick; drinking until the images of Amanda started to blur; drinking until he could somehow convince himself that none of this had happened—

But it had, of course.

And Sheriff Curry had been there to prove it had.

Sheriff Curry with his carbine; Sheriff Curry with his handcuffs; Sheriff Curry with his loudly banging cell door—

Now John Boyd sat here.

His father had to come.

Had to.

And soon.

John didn't know how much longer he could take being in this cell. It was getting small as a coffin. He felt—suffocated. Literally. He even starting panting, breathing in a labored way as if the cell were getting smaller, smaller . . .

Where the hell was his father, anyway?

He had to get here.

Soon.

"Have you ever met the boy's father, George Boyd, Mr. Ramsey?"

"Afraid I haven't."

"Well, let me tell you, he's quite a man. Quite a man."

"I'm sure he is."

"Without him, this area wouldn't be the richest in the

territory. When he got out here all you saw were Indians pissing in the creek."

"I hear he's quite a man," Ramsey said, hoping to stay neutral in this big buildup.

"And folks in these parts know how much we owe him."

Ramsey nodded.

"He built the bank and the bank made loans and the loans built a town. A little simplistic maybe but not by much. And that's how this part of the territory came into existence."

Ramsey said, "His son confessed, Mr. Stufflebeam."

Stufflebeam took the stogie from his mouth, looked at the end he'd richly wetted with his important, impatient mouth and then raised his eyes to Ramsey. "I understand there may have been some duress involved."

"None that I heard of."

Stufflebeam eyed him, the way a jeweler might assess a diamond. "Maybe if we'd go talk to the sheriff, he'd have a different story to tell."

"Sam himself was the one who told me that the boy confessed."

Stufflebeam eyed him, sighed, stared at his stogie again. "You walked around the town any this morning, Mr. Ramsey?"

"A little."

"You happen to notice five gunnies in town?"

"I did. In fact, I talked to one of them. Harry Robson."

"I spoke with Mr. Robson, too. He told me some things I'd just as soon not heard."

Ramsey didn't ask him what those things were.

"He told me that George Boyd will not permit—under any circumstances—his boy to be put on that train tonight."

"He pretty much told me the same thing."

Stufflebeam eyed him again. "Well, what are we going to do about that, Mr. Ramsey?"

"Afraid there isn't much we can do, Mr. Stufflebeam. The law's the law. The boy's got to be put on the train so he can stand trial."

"And those are your plans?"

"Those are my plans."

"Despite what you know about the boy's father?"

"Yessir."

"Despite what Harry Robson and his men will do to this town?"

"Yessir."

Stufflebeam frowned. "Are you thinking that the citizens of this town are going to help you, Mr. Ramsey?"

"I guess I hadn't given it much thought as yet."

"Well, they won't."

"It's their town. They've got more at stake here than I do."

"Yes, but they're also aware of who helped build this town. Who keeps on helping to build this town."

Now Ramsey's eyes appraised the older man. "How about if I was to help him to escape out the back door?"

"The boy, you mean?"

"Right."

Stufflebeam's face shone red with excitement. "You'd do that. I'd make sure you were repaid so's—"

Ramsey shook his head. "You'd really like me to do that, wouldn't you, Mr. Stufflebeam?"

"Of course I would. I know what we've got at stake here."

"You'd let law and order suffer because of some man's power?"

"If that's what it takes, yes." He frowned again. "I don't

want you to take this the wrong way, Mr. Ramsey, but the girl—"

"Amanda Sayles."

"Amanda Sayles, yessir. Well, she wasn't of the best stock. If you understand my meaning."

"I'm afraid I do."

"I'm not besmirching her reputation. I'm sure she was a fine and virtuous young girl, but—"

"But her parents aren't important—"

"Her father's a railroad worker—"

"And they probably live on the wrong side of town, right, Mr. Stufflebeam, and—"

Stufflebeam's fist came down like a sledgehammer on the top of Sheriff Curry's desk. "Do you think her life is worth what's going to happen to this town? Do you, Mr. Ramsey?"

Ramsey stood up. "I guess we've about said it all, Mr. Stufflebeam. Guess we might as well say good-bye."

Stufflebeam, exasperated, raised his black cane and shook it in Ramsey's face. "You'll regret your decision, Ramsey. Believe me, you'll regret it—and sooner than you think."

And with that, leaving cigar smoke and palpable rage in his wake, Stufflebeam left.

CHAPTER ★3★

1

He was afraid to die. Until the heart attacks started several years ago, Sheriff Sam Curry had always believed that when his time came, he would go soberly and without complaint into whatever death held for him. And certainly he would go without fear. Dying was a natural thing, he'd always told himself, and therefore nothing to be afraid of.

Now he knew better.

He lay in the bed his daughter Rita had freshened up for him an hour ago—clean sheets, a fluffed pillow, an open window with the pleasant smell of a warm autumn morning coming through it—and knew that he was no better, no braver than any other pilgrim who'd ever trekked the planet.

He was afraid to die.

He hoped it would be in his sleep, when he couldn't say or do anything that would show Rita how afraid he really was. Maybe if he was strong about death, he could inspire her to be strong about death, too. Seemed this was the best gift a parent could give his offspring.

He was thinking all these things when Edwin Stufflebeam appeared in his bedroom doorway like an apparition. An unwelcome one. Stufflebeam was one of Congreve's few prominent citizens with whom Curry had never been able to get along. No open hostility, of course—they were both good at politics—but their voices took on a certain edge whenever they addressed each other.

Stufflebeam's usually hard and demanding voice took on softer tones now as he looked at Curry in his bed. Perhaps he was seeing himself in a similar situation not too many years from now.

"Morning, Sam."

"Morning, Edwin."

"Rita said I could see you for a few minutes if I didn't upset you."

Curry smiled ironically. "You upset me, Edwin? Hard to imagine."

Stufflebeam returned the chill smile and entered the room. He seemed slightly afraid, as if Curry's ailment might be contagious. He glanced around the small, handsome room at the beautiful mahogany furnishings and the brass bed and the Civil War photographs on the east wall and said, "I just visited with your friend over at the sheriff's department. Ramsey."

"A fine man, isn't he?"

"At any other time, I suppose he would be."

Curry knew what was coming, of course. "At any other time?"

Stufflebeam nodded solemnly. "George Boyd summoned me out to his ranch in the middle of the night."

"That wasn't a surprise, was it?"

"No. But I'll tell you what was a surprise—how pissed he is, Sam. It's like he's—insane or something. I don't know how else to describe him." Stufflebeam set his jaw. "He wants his boy back, Sam. Now."

"You know that isn't possible."

"We've got to make it possible, Sam. For the sake of this town."

"Can't do it."

Stufflebeam stared at him. He looked old and tired, not his usual imperious self. "What if it could be arranged that the boy escaped and that nobody was held responsible?"

Curry stared back at him. "Nope, Edwin. Wouldn't be right. He killed that girl and that's that."

"You wouldn't lose face, Sam. Nobody would ever think of holding you accountable."

A breeze billowed the sheer white curtains. The smells of autumn were sweet and rich in the room. Curry said, "We're supposed to be civilized here, Edwin. Law and order. That's the basis of civilization. Once you start letting killers go free, no matter who their daddies are, you lose everything you've worked to establish. Can't you see that?"

"He's got his gunnies here."

"I'm aware of that."

"A lot of innocent people could get killed."

"I'm aware of that, too."

"Sam, you—"

"Mr. Stufflebeam."

The interrupting voice was soft as lute music on the warm morning. And with it, Rita Curry stepped into the room and hushed him with a long, slender finger put to her pretty mouth. "I thought you agreed not to upset him."

"I tried not to."

She looked at her father. "He told me he just wanted to see how you were doing."

Curry laughed. "Edwin means well, honey. He just can't get used to the idea that somebody would actually say no to George Boyd."

Rita went to the head of the bed, eased her father's head up, picked up the pillow, fluffed it and put it back in place. "You rest now, all right?"

Curry waved to Stufflebeam. "Actually, Edwin, I enjoyed seeing you. You got my thoughts off morbid things and I appreciate it."

Stufflebeam smiled tightly. "I'll say a prayer for you, Sam."

Curry laughed again. "Why don't you make that two prayers?"

On the doorstep, as she was letting Stufflebeam out, Rita said, "You promised not to upset him, Mr. Stufflebeam. Yet you went in there and discussed business with him anyway." Others in town might be intimidated by Edwin Stufflebeam's powerful presence, but not Rita Curry. Maybe being a very attractive "old maid" of thirty-one gave her a boldness that other women—concerned about their responsibilities— lacked. Right now, her anger was obvious.

Stufflebeam said, "I'm sorry if I made you angry, Miss Curry."

"It's just that you broke your promise."

Then her anger subsided. "I suppose you were only doing what you felt you had to."

"I'm concerned for the town, Miss Curry."

"I know."

"Can't you talk to him?"

GUNDOWN 27

She looked back to the bedroom. "I—I'm not sure it's my place."

"Then you agree with me that the Boyd boy should be let go?"

"I don't want to see the town torn apart."

He touched her with surprising gentleness on the arm. "Won't you talk with him, Miss Curry? Reason with him? Please? For everybody's sake?"

She looked at him and sighed. "I'll think it over, Mr. Stufflebeam. Good day."

Then she went back into the house and quietly closed the door behind her.

2

After Stufflebeam left the sheriff's office, Ramsey decided to go in the back and meet the prisoner John Boyd. But just as he put a hand on the door leading to the cells, the front door opened and there stood a tiny old lady in a sunbonnet and matching gingham dress. She had tears in her eyes. She looked straight at Ramsey and said, "It's Calico."

"Calico?"

"My cat."

"I see."

"He's in the tree."

"I'm sorry."

"All because of Clyde."

"Clyde?"

"My dog."

"Oh."

"Today's Calico's birthday and Clyde's just jealous."

"I see."

"But Calico's so scared I can't get her down from the tree."

"And you'd like me to—"

"Oh, if you only would. If you only would." The little old lady put her hands together and sort of swooned.

Despite the presence of a killer in the cells and four gunnies waiting for some bloodshed, life in Congreve went on, treed kitty cats and all.

Ramsey made sure everything was secured and then followed the little old lady out the door.

Calico turned out to be a Russian blue, which made her name totally mysterious and inappropriate, and Clyde turned out to be an appealing, flop-eared beagle who lay lazily at the base of a big elm and let loose a tired-sounding bark every half minute or so.

"See?" the little old lady said. "You can tell he's jealous."

"Right," Ramsey said.

He hadn't climbed a tree in years. Halfway up this one, he remembered why. Because it was a tricky and risky proposition, and because you can fall on your can and break some serious bones.

The kitty cat was very cute and scared looking, all hunched up in the Y of a large, leafy limb.

It took one, two, three tries, but Ramsey finally got hold of the kitty cat and was able to stroke her long enough to hold on and pick her up and carry her gently downward.

Before he'd reached the ground, Ramsey heard the little old lady making cooing and doving sounds with the kitty cat, telling her how happy she was that this was her birthday and all that.

Ramsey handed the kitty cat over to the woman as if he were presenting her with a door prize.

By this time, Clyde was sound asleep. He didn't so much as open an eye now that Calico was down.

The little old lady, kitty cat tucked into her arm, leaned over and said to the snoring dog, "You bad boy, you bad boy. Now you be good."

Ramsey couldn't imagine this dog as any sort of "bad boy" at all, but then it really wasn't any of his business.

The little old lady asked him if he'd like some cake and coffee, but he passed and started back down the shady residential dirt street to the four-block business district.

He was nearing the sheriff's office when he saw them.

They stood under the overhang of the town's largest hotel. There was a fat but hard-looking man in a black suit and three gunnies of various sizes and ages. Like most gunnies, they managed to exude violence and stupidity in equal parts.

And they saw him, too.

They stood staring at him as he made his way past them back to the sheriff's office.

He was just glad they hadn't seen him bringing a kitty cat down from a tree. It might have given them the wrong impression.

Inside the office, he found Rita Curry waiting for him.

While she was an attractive woman, Ramsey sensed why she was unmarried. She was aloof to the point of coldness. He sensed she didn't like being this way but didn't know how to help herself. She looked at him now with tired, worried eyes.

"Morning, Matt."

"Morning, Rita. Care for some coffee?"

"Please."

Ramsey poured them two cups. "How's your father doing?"

"About the same."

He handed her a cup of steaming coffee. He sat on the edge of the desk and faced her. "Anything I can do for you?"

She looked at him levelly. "Yes. I'd like you to let John Boyd go."

He sighed. "I'm surprised, Rita. A daughter of Sam Curry wanting me to do something like that."

"It's the only sensible thing, Matt."

"It may be sensible but it sure isn't right. He's a confessed murderer."

"It's going to start and very soon."

"What is?"

"The trouble. That's why those four men are here."

"I know. And I'm ready for it."

"There's just you and Quinn, Matt. Nobody else in this town will help you."

"I sure hope that isn't true. For the town's sake."

"They owe George Boyd too much. And they're afraid of him."

"Sam hasn't changed his mind, has he?"

She smiled with just a trace of bitterness. "Old Mr. Law 'n' Order himself? Not hardly." She looked down at her hands in her lap. Then she looked up at Ramsey. "I love him, Matt."

"I know."

"Won't you help?"

"I thought I was."

"You know what I mean. It shouldn't matter to you if John Boyd goes free. It isn't your town. You don't have to live here."

Ramsey shook his head. "I can't do it, Rita."

She stood up, an old woman before her time. " '*Won't* do it' is what you mean."

He watched her walk over to the front door. "Say hello to Sam for me."

She said nothing. She left.

He was just turning back to the cell door, thinking he'd finally get a look at John Boyd, when he heard gunfire from up the street.

He grabbed a carbine and took off running.

3

By the time he reached the small crowd, the gunfire had stopped.

A small man in everyday gray work clothes stood in front of the four gunnies. The onlookers seemed both fascinated and afraid of what they were seeing.

Robson reached out and slapped the small man so hard, the man nearly went over backward. With his slight build, sallow skin and gray hair, it was clear he was no match for the fat man.

Then Robson snatched the small man's carbine, raised a knee and snapped the carbine in two pieces. These he threw on the dusty ground.

He grabbed the small man, jerking him. He slapped him once more. Finished, Robson shoved the small man into the crowd.

Ramsey, just arriving, pushed his way through the onlookers and went up to the fat man. "You have any reason to take a man's rifle and break it in two?"

The fat man nodded. "I'm glad you got here, Sheriff. I

was afraid I might have to shoot Sayles here. I'm afraid he's determined to kill me."

"Apparently you didn't hear my question."

Robson looked at his four gunnies and smiled. "Oh, I heard all right, Sheriff. I was just hoping one of these fine citizens would speak up in my defense."

An old man said, "Sayles tried to shoot him." The old man looked as if he resented having to speak up for somebody like Robson.

"And that's just the way it happened, Ramsey," Robson said. "We were just having ourselves a nice little conversation, and here comes Sayles, walks right up to me, and puts his carbine in my face. Lucky for me I had the presence of mind to take his gun from him."

The gunnies smiled.

The crowd started to fade, leaving Robert Sayles alone.

"Is this true?" Ramsey said to Sayles.

Sayles nodded, dropped his head.

Ramsey bent down and picked up the two pieces of the carbine. He took them over and handed them to Sayles. "Go over on that sidewalk and wait for me. You hear?"

"You're sidin' with him, ain't you?" Sayles said. Anger replaced sorrow in the man's eyes.

"If you tried to shoot him, I guess I don't have much choice, do I?"

"Don't you know who he is? Don't you know why he's here?"

"You just go over there and stand," Ramsey said.

Sayles looked at Robson. "You try'n bust that boy out, Robson, and next time I'll kill you for sure. It don't mean nothin' to you, but that boy killed my daughter and he deserves to die. No matter who his father is. You understand me?"

Robson said to Ramsey, "I don't know what the hell that old bastard's talking about. Do you, Sheriff?"

Ramsey pointed to the sidewalk across the street. Sayles reluctantly went over there. Every few feet, he'd look over his shoulder to glare at Robson.

Robson said, "You change your mind about that money, Ramsey? I'm still willing to give it to you."

"I thought maybe you'd changed your mind, Robson. Looked around this nice little town and decided to ride back to George Boyd and tell him there are a lot of decent people here."

"A man isn't real appreciative of a town that's going to hang his son."

Robson nodded across the street. His gaze had hardened considerably. His ironic manner was gone. "That little bastard comes around me with a gun again, I'll kill him right in his tracks, Ramsey. And you'd better convince him I mean it."

"I'll convince him."

"Right now I feel the need for a drink, Ramsey. Same place as before. If you change your mind about the money, I'll be waiting there." He glanced around the sunny street. Everything looked scrubbed and tidy. Not even the fly-buzzed horseshit in the middle of the street smelled too bad right now.

"See you later, Ramsey," Robson said, and he strolled away, his gunnies bobbing after him like kids around a dad they hadn't seen for a time.

"You ever have kids, Ramsey?"
"Nope."
"Then you can't understand."
"I can understand some at least."

"That man wants to free the punk who killed my daughter."

"I realize that, Sayles."

"And I ain't going to let him."

The sorrow was gone again. The anger had taken him. Ramsey supposed it was a good thing. Anger allowed you at least a temporary respite from grief. With sorrow, all you could do was sink lower.

They sat in a small café that smelled of coffee, apple pie and roast beef. There was a red and white checkered oilcloth on the table that was sleek under Ramsey's elbows. He had a cigarette going, and Sayles was smoking his third. Ramsey figured that the deputy was back at the jail by now to keep tabs on the prisoner.

Ramsey said, "He'll kill you."

"Maybe right now I don't give a damn if he kills me. Maybe right now all I care about is stopping him from helping John escape." His gaze softened. The sorrow was back. "You didn't know her, Ramsey."

Ramsey sighed. He didn't know what else to do, to say.

"She was pretty and gentle and educated. She got through the sixth grade. She could read. A lot of nights her mother and I would sit at the table and she'd read stories to us." He started crying then in the hard, abrupt way of men. "And then John has to go and—"

Sayles's small hands made small fists.

"I'm sorry, Sayles," Ramsey said.

Sayles snuffled his tears. "All I can ask for now is justice, Ramsey. Just because I'm a poor man don't mean that he shouldn't stand trial."

"He's going to stand trial."

"And be hanged."

"I'm not the jury, Sayles. My part in all this is to get him on that train tonight."

"Then you're not going to throw in with Robson?"

"Nope."

"You promise?"

Ramsey laughed. "You want me to sign a contract, Sayles?"

For the first time since he'd met the man, he saw Sayles smile. "I wouldn't mind that at all."

Ramsey drained his coffee. "I've got to get back to the jail, Sayles. But you remember what I said. Don't go anywhere near Robson. You understand?"

Sayles shrugged.

"He'll kill you, Sayles. With no hesitation. And if you're armed, he'll be in the right."

Sayles looked up at the clock on the wall. "I wish that train would get here."

Ramsey stood up, tugged on his hat. "You can't wish it any more than I do, Sayles."

4

His father had taken him to a hanging once. John Boyd wasn't sure how old he'd been—seven, eight—but he did recall one thing clearly; the way the crowd obviously enjoyed itself. Except for the times he went to the fair, he'd never seen so many people so happy. The lawmen didn't bring up the condemned man for a long time. It was almost as if they were trying to build up the excitement within the crowd higher and higher, the way showmen did.

John remembered wondering if the man would be scared. He'd heard ranch hands talk of a few men who'd been defiant, spitting on the crowd below or loudly cursing the hangman. But then, as he stood there in the cool autumn sunlight, the smell of fresh-sawn pine from the scaffolding sharp in his nose, he saw the condemned man for the first time, and he knew that what he was about to see was going to be terrible.

Two men guided the prisoner up the steps. The man could barely walk; indeed, he fell down to his knees twice before reaching the top. He was crying. Oh, maybe not sobbing out loud, but tears were running down his unshaven cheeks, and his lower lip was trembling wildly. As they slipped the noose around his neck, he started praying very loudly, as if the Lord needed to be addressed in shouts. Then, mercifully, they slipped the black hood over his face. Just as the trap door snapped open, the man let out a cry for help that John Boyd was to remember for many years.

Now, all these years later, he sat in a cold, hard cell contemplating his own eventual death by hanging.

Was there a special place in hell for men who'd died with the executioner's black hood over their faces?

Just then the cell-block door opened. The deputy Dennis Quinn came in.

"Morning, John."

"Morning, Dennis."

That was the hell of it. How nice people were in the jail. He couldn't tell if it was because his old man was George Boyd or if they just naturally treated everybody this way.

"You finally get rid of that hangover?" Quinn asked from the other side of the bars.

John even managed a small grin for him. "Guess I did at that."

Quinn put the key in the lock.

For a wild moment, heart hammering, John wondered if he was going to be released. Maybe his father's influence had—

GUNDOWN

But Quinn only said, "You've got visitors, John."

"Visitors?"

"Lawyers. Stoddard and Coleman."

"Oh." You could hear John's voice—and hopes—sink. "My father's lawyers."

"Right. I told them they could have half an hour with you."

"Thanks."

"Sure."

Quinn walked back to the front of the cells and said to somebody unseen in the outer office, "You can come in now, gentlemen."

And so they did.

Stoddard and Coleman were about what you'd expect in a town this size, men got up in three-piece suits, homburg hats and an almost impressive air of self-importance. Their chief expertise was bribing territorial officials for their clients.

They made neat contrasts, the two, Stoddard short, chunky and aggressive, Coleman tall, lanky and mild.

Both men carried with them cups of hickory coffee. It smelled good in the dank air of the cell.

"Might be better if you had a little company in one of the other cells," Amos Stoddard said.

"I like it fine this way."

Karl Coleman looked around. "They keep it clean, anyway. Guess you have to give Sam Curry credit for being a good lawman."

Stoddard snapped, "I don't have to give Sam Curry credit for anything."

That was another thing about the two. They bickered like a married couple who didn't get along.

Coleman said, "How've they been treating you?"

"Fine."

"Food good?"

"Yep."

"Plenty of blankets?"

John Boyd nodded.

"They treating you mean about the killing or anything?"

John Boyd stared at Coleman and said, "What're all these questions about?"

Stoddard, instead of Coleman, answered. "Well, we hear otherwise."

"Otherwise?"

"Hear you haven't been treated so well."

"That just isn't true."

Stoddard looked at Coleman. In a soft voice he said to John Boyd, "We hear that Curry beat you before you made your confession."

"No."

"You think about it, John," Coleman said. "You think hard about it. Maybe you were so drunk you don't remember being beaten."

"But—"

"If they didn't have your confession to go on," Stoddard said, "they wouldn't have much at all."

Coleman said, "And if we were able to prove that you'd been beaten by Curry—"

"Show that you had marks from that beating—"

"But I don't. I—"

"But maybe you just haven't looked hard enough," Stoddard said, and with that he slipped from inside his suit coat a long piece of cloth-bound metal that was a kind of homemade blackjack.

You could inflict a lot of injury with a weapon like that.

Stoddard said, "Coleman's going to watch the door up there. And I'm going to get in the cell with you." He smiled.

"Deputy Quinn was nice enough to unlock it for me."

Coleman said, "All you have to do is pull up your shirt, John."

"And not yell," Stoddard said. "No matter how much I hurt you, you'll have to be quiet. You understand?"

John Boyd thought of the condemned man crying out for help just before they pulled the black hood over his face.

He didn't want to end up that way.

And if it meant enduring Stoddard's pain here . . .

"All right," he said, and he pushed open the cell door for Stoddard to come inside.

CHAPTER
★4★

1

An old black man was washing down a tired roan inside a dusty rope corral behind the livery stable. The man stroked the horse as he used the brush on him. He also whispered things in the horse's ear. The horse looked grateful for the company.

Ramsey stood outside the corral and said, "Excuse me."

The black man turned around. "Yessir?"

"Would you be Morty?"

The black man grinned with no teeth. "No, and I don't reckon Morty would appreciate that question, either. I'm Eddie."

"You tell me where I can find Morty?"

The man nodded to an outhouse downslope from where they stood. It was a narrow, shacky structure constructed of rotting boards. An unlikely blue jay was perched on the edge of the outhouse roof.

Eddie smiled again. "Taking his constitutional." He nodded to Ramsey's badge. "You're Curry's friend, huh?"

"That's right."

"Heard you was in the war together."

"Yep."

"On the gray side."

Ramsey nodded. "Nothin' personal."

Eddie eyed him suspiciously. "Guess not." He pointed to the back end of the livery stable. "Small office up there. Some good strong coffee brewin', too. Why don't you wait up there for him?"

"So you're Ramsey?"

"Right."

"Sam always talks about you."

Ramsey smiled. "In civil terms, I hope."

"Hell, glowing terms. According to him, you were the bravest man in the entire Confederacy."

Ramsey shook his head. "Sam likes his tales."

Morty was not the kind of man you usually found taking the role of the town smithy. Instead of a squat body with bulging muscles, he was tall, and lanky, and had a lean, angular face with warm brown eyes. He was also bald.

"I hear some of Boyd's men came to town," Morty said.

They were in his messy office. His rolltop desk overflowed with papers and the spittoon smelled as if it hadn't been cleaned out in a long, long time.

"Then you know why I'm here," Ramsey said.

"You want me to help you round up some deputies?"

"Right."

Morty shook his shiny head. "Won't be easy."

"So I'm told."

"Boyd can be one mean son of a bitch, let me tell you. Especially where Junior's involved." He smirked. "I went to school with Junior. He's a real asshole."

"Right now I'm more concerned with Harry Robson and his boys."

"Robson, huh?" Morty whistled.

Ramsey disregarded the sound. "Half a dozen men should do it. I've got four carbines at the jail. I'll need two more."

"Guns you can get plenty of. It's the men that'll be the problem."

"There aren't six men in this town who hate Boyd enough to stand up to him?"

"Oh, there are a lot more than that. But there may not be six who are brave enough."

Morty went over and sat down at his desk. He pushed aside several piles of paper. From beneath them he took an old Navy Colt. He examined the gun and shook his head. "Never thought I'd use this old boy again."

"I can count on you?"

"On me, yes. I don't know what kind of luck I'm going to have with the others, though."

"Do your best."

"I'll try."

Ramsey finished his coffee. "Say, everybody's mentioned you as Morty, but nobody's ever told me your last name."

"You won't want to hear it."

"No?"

"No. It's Boyd."

Before Ramsey could say anything, Morty laughed and said, "George Boyd is my uncle. But it's nothing to worry about. I hate the old bastard. I'm the civic-minded type. I want to see Congreve grow up, not stay on as his private fiefdom."

"You'd actually fight his men?"

Morty patted the Navy Colt. "I'd consider it a pleasure. It's time somebody took care of my uncle—and my cousin John. Though to be honest, Ramsey, I don't think John's too bad a guy. It's just the way he was raised. His father wanted him to rule this whole valley. John didn't want to. He just wanted to be a normal boy, like the rest of us. He started getting into trouble so his father couldn't count on him. If that makes any sense."

Ramsey shook his head. "I could feel a lot sorrier for John if he hadn't killed that girl."

Morty grimaced. "Yeah. I guess I could, too."

Ramsey tugged on his hat. "I'll be back in a couple hours to see how your recruiting is going."

"See you then, Ramsey."

2

The trick was not to scream. If he screamed then the deputy would come in and see what was happening and would stop it.

His hands gripped the bars as Stoddard took the sap and worked over John Boyd's ribs and sides.

Boyd had to bite down so hard on his lip, he drew blood.

He glanced over his shoulder at Stoddard.

The lawyer didn't look as if he were enjoying himself, anyway.

"Just a couple more times," Stoddard said.

And brought the sap across Boyd's cheek.

Boyd moaned but kept himself from screaming.

"We've got to make it look real, son. Otherwise Judge McBain won't side with us. You know how he is—the law goes first, even before George Boyd."

"Just a few more times," Coleman said.

This time Stoddard got John Boyd to turn around in the cell and face him.

Stoddard brought the sap across the bridge of Boyd's nose.

Boyd fell to the floor as if he'd been shot, his hands covering his face.

The pain was incredible, and he did not like the taste of blood in his throat or the hot, sticky feel of it on his face.

"Sorry, son," Stoddard said again.

They helped him to his feet and laid him back on his cot and got him a rag for his nose.

"Now it's very important that you keep your face covered up till we get back here with the judge," Stoddard said. "We don't want Ramsey to know what we're up to until McBain is with us. You understand?"

Behind his bloody rag, John Boyd nodded.

"Now we're going to walk up front and have the deputy see us out, so you just roll over on your side facing the wall there and don't let him get a look at your face. All right?"

Repeating himself this way, Stoddard sounded a lot like a parent talking to a particularly dumb child. This said a lot about the way he regarded John Boyd.

Boyd rolled over, doing as the two lawyers told him.

He heard the cell door creak open and then creak closed again, and then he heard the two men walk up to the front of the jail in their heavy boots.

Out on the street, John Boyd could hear the heavy, late-morning traffic of ore wagons and stagecoaches and buckboards laden with various kinds of produce.

He wanted to be out there with the people. In the sunlight. Walking to a saloon. Anticipating the girls and the cards and the fun.

He tried not to think about Amanda Sayles.

How much he'd loved her.

Or what he'd done to her two nights ago.

He tried not to think about that at all.

After a while, John Boyd still on his side, the deputy came back. He smelled of pipe tobacco.

He came up to the cell door and inserted a metal key from a clanking metal key ring and locked up the cell again.

The deputy said, "You asleep?"

"Resting is all," John Boyd said, taking the rag from his bloody nose so he could talk.

"You all right?"

"Huh?"

"You all right? You sound kind of funny."

"I'm fine."

John Boyd could feel the deputy working him over with his eyes, trying to figure out exactly what was going on.

The deputy gripped the cell bars and tugged hard, making sure the door was locked.

"You want some lunch?"

"Guess not."

"You sure? Café's got fried chicken for lunch."

"Thanks anyway."

The deputy laughed. "Maybe this is my lucky day."

"Huh?"

"I've never heard a Boyd say 'Thank you' to anybody for anything."

John Boyd said nothing.

The deputy tried the door again. Locked.

"I think you're making a mistake about the chicken," the deputy said.

John Boyd just shrugged his shoulders.

At last, the deputy went away, leaving John Boyd with his painful face and ribs and his terrible memories.

The hell of it was, he really had loved Amanda.

Had planned to marry her.

Have children. And then two nights ago . . .

Then he knew a different kind of pain—remorse. If there was one thing he wanted to take back, it was the other night and what he'd done to Amanda.

At first, he wasn't even aware of it, his crying. But gradually his shoulders started to shake and tears mixed with blood on his cheeks, and then there was just this awful ache in his chest.

She'd been so beautiful; so trusting; so good . . .

Images of her head lolling dead on her shoulder; of her hands trying to protect her face as he attacked her; of her lying there in the moonlight like an innocent young girl a terrible beast had savaged . . .

After a time, his tears and the physical pain exhausting him, he slept.

3

Judge Cletus George McBain had come to this district fourteen years ago determined to impress the rule of law on a town that had previously used lynching as its chief means of keeping the peace. McBain held court three days a week in a small building made of newly sawn pine, and with a permanent scaffolding out back. On nice days, McBain was known to fly the hangman's noose, even when a hanging wasn't scheduled, so people would pay heed to the notion of swift and terrible justice. It was said that McBain liked to fly the noose the way others liked to fly the flag.

People soon understood what McBain—now known as Maximum McBain—was all about. For the smallest infraction of law, you would be forced to pay the largest price. Congreve soon enough became a law-abiding town, except for the vagaries of George Boyd, who was so powerful that even Maximum McBain had trouble making the law stick. It was widely known that McBain was biding his time until he could win a crucial confrontation with his nemesis Boyd.

Karl Coleman thought about all this as he and his law partner Stoddard walked from the jail to McBain's offices. He knew that McBain would be reluctant to go along with their proposal that young Boyd had been beaten and should therefore be released into Coleman's custody until a trial date was set, but Coleman believed that once McBain saw the bruises, he'd have no choice but to go along.

For a man nicknamed Maximum, Cletus McBain was an unimpressive looking man. He looked, as one wag had put it, like a bullfrog who was trying hard to fart. Not even in his robes did his small, dumpy body and bulging, froggy features look impressive.

Coleman thought all these uncharitable thoughts as he stood in front of McBain's formidable mahogany desk in an office right outside the courtroom. Stoddard was downstairs and outside. McBain hated Stoddard so passionately the lawyers knew better than to bring him along on so delicate a mission.

"Morning, Judge."

McBain was pretending to be overwhelmingly busy just

to irritate Coleman. Finally, he looked up from his legal documents. "Yes?"

"I'd like you to accompany me to the jail."

"Might I ask why?"

"I'd like you to look at John Boyd."

"I've seen John Boyd all I care to."

"At his wounds."

"What wounds?"

"The wounds Sam Curry inflicted on him to get a confession."

"Now there's a crock of shit and you know it." This kind of language never fazed Maximum McBain, not even when he was wearing his judicial robes.

"You may choose not to believe it. That doesn't mean it didn't happen."

"Are you still floating that bullshit idea that young Boyd is innocent?"

"He is."

"He confessed."

"But only after he was beaten."

"Sam Curry isn't that kind of lawman."

"He was that night."

McBain sneered. "This was Stoddard's idea, wasn't it?"

"What idea?"

"To trump up a charge like this."

"As an officer of the court, Your Honor, it's your sworn duty to accompany me to the jail."

"Sworn duty my ass."

"You won't say that after you see the prisoner."

"The hell I won't."

"Your Honor—"

McBain shook his head. He looked as if he'd just been forced to eat a rattlesnake. He waved a tiny hand in Karl

Coleman's direction. "At least don't make me listen to any more of your lies. Let's just go over there and get the damn thing over with so I can tell you no and get back to my work."

Karl Coleman was about to say something else.

Maximum McBain waved for him to be silent.

4

Sometimes, tragedy made unpopular people popular, least for a few hours or days. A man nobody usually spoke to often became the center of attention when something terrible befell a member of his family.

Sometimes, anyway, but such was not the case with wary little Robert Sayles. A railroad man by trade, Sayles was the sort of whiny drunk other drunks avoided. All Sayles ever did was bemoan his lot. His wife had died young. His crops had gone bad when he'd farmed. His carpentry clients were always late paying him. Then there was the railroad. Bitch, bitch, bitch. You could be in the best mood in the world, and in the course of one schooner of beer, Robert Sayles could put you in the mood for a funeral. He couldn't help it—he probably wasn't even aware he was doing it. It was just the way he was. It was probably in his blood.

So when his beautiful young daughter was killed by the Boyd boy, people really started avoiding Sayles. He was bad enough when he *didn't* have anything to piss and moan about—imagine what he'd be like with a dead daughter on his hands.

So now he stood at the end of the long plank bar in this grimy railroad tavern down by the roundhouse. He was well aware that the other men were avoiding him, just as people had avoided him all his life, just a quick nod and maybe an appropriately mournful glance—and then they were gone to their friends, talking and laughing as if his daughter hadn't been murdered just a few days ago.

Alcohol had no effect on him today. Usually a couple of schooners soused him up a little. He'd always attributed this to his small size.

Standing here now, ordering another schooner from the barkeep who was just as eager to get away from gloomy Sayles as everybody else, he thought again of the carbine he'd seen in the window of the general store this morning.

Of course, there was no way he could stroll in there and buy it. Lem, the owner, would run straight-ass to Matt Ramsey and tell him all about the purchase, and then Ramsey would come looking for him and take the weapon away.

No, what Sayles was thinking about was tonight. After dark. Given his carpentry experience, jimmying open a door lock was no problem.

Then he could sneak in on cat feet and snatch the weapon from the window and then—

Then he could take care of John Boyd.

He had never felt manly, Sayles hadn't. He was not only diminutive of size, he was also fine boned like a woman, his wrists and fingers particularly delicate. He had never felt strong or purposeful or able to defend his own honor or his family's honor. He had lived his life at the mercy and whims of men more powerful . . . and now that his daughter had been killed, he realized he could no longer afford the luxury of weakness.

Now he had to be a man like those men he feared and envied.

But all this thinking, all this planning was likely to come

to nothing because he knew that he would never be lucky, enough to get the weapon and kill Boyd. Sayles just wasn't that kind of man. Oh, he'd shot his mouth off to Harry Robson earlier this morning, but Robson had easily turned him aside, breaking his rifle in the process. No, he would be left with a life of bitterness and anger about which he could do nothing. Nothing.

"You get ready for another one, Mr. Sayles. I'd like to buy it for you."

Sayles turned to his right. A tall man in a three-piece suit stood there. He had the look and demeanor of a city man, yet there was something almost raw and powerful about him, too. Then Sayles recognized him. "I'll be damned."

The tall man put out his hand. "You remember me, then?"

"I sure as hell do. Thomas Peck."

Peck nodded. "I came when I heard about Amanda."

Sayles sighed and shook his head. "John Boyd killed her."

"Yes."

"And knowing how his father operates, I'll bet he gets away with it."

Peck stared at him steadily. "You'd like to kill John Boyd, wouldn't you?"

Sayles had the uneasy feeling that this rangy young man was reading his mind.

Peck said, "I loved her, Mr. Sayles. But I guess you knew that. I courted her for two years before Boyd came into the picture and then—"

Peck shook his head, raised his glass and downed some straight whiskey.

Sayles remembered the young man's heartbreak. He'd felt sorry for Peck, who had obviously and deeply loved Amanda. But she'd let her head be turned by Boyd's good looks and money, and Peck had been banished. He'd gone to work as an inspector for the railroad, a job that took him far away and kept him far away. But Sayles could see now that Peck still loved his daughter. The pain on his face matched Sayles's own.

Peck said, "I'd like to help you kill him, Mr. Sayles. That's why I came back to town."

5

The coffee had started to get to Ramsey. Five cups so far today, and it was scarcely past noon. He had many hours to go before the train that was to take John Boyd away would pull into Congreve's small depot.

Finishing the fifth cup now, he said, "You want to take a little time off and go see your wife and kids?"

Deputy Quinn nodded. "I'd appreciate that if you wouldn't mind, Matt."

"Be my guest."

"If my wife made some of her good biscuits, I'll bring you a few back."

Ramsey smiled. "Sounds good." He nodded to the door leading to the cells. "I guess I'd better go back and introduce myself to the prisoner, seeing as how I'll be the one putting him on the train tonight."

Deputy Quinn nodded, picked up the newspaper he'd been reading and then left the office.

Ramsey followed him over to the front door, locking it behind him.

Then he went back to the cells.

No matter how you tried to fix up jails, Ramsey thought, no matter how much soap and water and paint you used, they were still jails—cages for human beings. They smelled of sorrow and remorse. And they also smelled of hatred and rage, of men desperate enough to do anything.

This particular jail was shadowy and damp. The walls were covered with dirty words that had been carved in them with spoons and forks. Some of the cots sagged in the middle from too-heavy prisoners. The sky seen through the small oblong windows looked enticingly blue.

Ramsey went down to the last cell and looked in.

John Boyd was lying down, facing away from Ramsey. All Ramsey could see was the young man's back.

"Boyd?"

Boyd said nothing.

"Boyd, I thought I'd introduce myself. I'm Matt Ramsey. I'm spelling Sheriff Curry to take you to the train tonight."

Boyd said nothing.

And Ramsey knew something was wrong.

"Boyd," he said, a little more urgently now.

He'd just taken the loop of keys from his belt when somebody started banging loudly on the front door.

"Damn," he said under his breath.

The thunderous knocking came again.

He slipped the keys back on his belt and started out of the back end of the jail.

The front office was a good five degrees warmer, and it smelled much better than the jail, too.

As he made his way to the front door, Ramsey felt grateful to be in good, warm sunlight again.

Three men stood in the front door. One of them wore the black robes of justice. The other two were dressed in expensive city clothes and didn't look as if they worked too hard at being humble.

"These two jackasses," said the man in the black robes,

"are trying to convince me that Sheriff Curry beat a confession out of John Boyd. Do you know anything about that?"

Then the short, chunky man pushed his hand out. "I'm Judge McBain, and these two whores are the lawyers George Boyd uses in this town."

Ramsey almost smiled at the smaller man's spluttering anger. There was something comic about it.

Stoddard and Coleman then introduced themselves, too.

"I visited the prisoner this morning," Coleman said quietly. "And he looked bad enough to be in a hospital."

"Is that true, Ramsey?" the judge wanted to know.

"I can't say. I haven't talked to the prisoner."

"I'd say let's go take a look at him right now," Stoddard said.

Judge McBain glowered when Stoddard spoke. Obviously, he detested this man.

The four of them went inside the office, then through the door leading to the cells, then back into the jail itself.

"This place could stand a little sunlight," Stoddard said.

"I don't worry about coddling criminals," Judge McBain shot back.

When they reached Boyd's cell, the man was still lying down, with his back facing them.

"You've got company, Boyd. Time to sit up," Ramsey said.

Stoddard said, "That's right, John. Why don't you turn around here and talk to us?"

John Boyd rolled slowly, painfully off the cot. First he got himself turned around and sat on the edge of the cot, and then he very carefully set one foot down on the floor and started to pull himself up.

"My God," said Karl Coleman. "Look at him."

There was no mistaking what Coleman was referring to, Ramsey saw. Somebody had worked John Boyd over very well. His nose was smashed and bloody, and his cheeks and forehead showed dark bruises. The way he grimaced every time he stepped down, it was easy to guess that his ribs had been damaged, too.

"My God," Karl Coleman said again, just in case nobody had heard him the first time.

Ramsey got the cell door open.

Judge McBain went inside to inspect the prisoner himself.

Just before he went in, though, he glared at Ramsey. Glared hard. As if Ramsey had had something to do with this.

"You sit down over there and let me have a look at you," McBain said, helping Boyd sit on the edge of the cot.

Then, much in the way a doctor would, McBain looked him over.

About halfway through his examination, McBain said, "What do you know about this, Ramsey?"

"Nothing."

"Bullshit."

Now it was Ramsey's turn to glare. Right at the two lawyers. "Sam Curry wouldn't do anything like this."

But despite his words, Stoddard and Coleman were looking damn smug. "I'd suggest that you turn the prisoner over to us," Coleman said, "and let us take him over to the hospital." Then he looked at Ramsey and shook his head. "It's obvious he isn't safe in this jail."

Behind them, Ramsey heard somebody coming into the jail. He turned to see Deputy Quinn. Even in the shadows, it was easy to see that Quinn was bringing bad news of some kind. Ramsey wondered what was wrong.

Before giving the deputy the chance to speak, however, Ramsey said, "Quinn was here when Sam was questioning Boyd. Here, deputy, you know anything about this?"

Quinn came up closer to the cell door and peeked inside. He whistled low at the human wreck who sat before him. "When'd this happen? He was fine an hour ago."

Judge McBain said, "So this didn't happen the other night?"

"Nope," Quinn said. Then he looked at the two lawyers. "I'm sure it happened this morning, when these two gentlemen came to visit Boyd here."

Judge McBain held up a single index finger. It had blood smeared all over it. "That explains it, then."

"Explains what?" Ramsey said.

"Why the blood from Boyd's nose is still so fresh." He smiled coldly at the lawyers. "You should be able to do better than this, considering all the money Boyd pays you." Then he stood up and looked down at John Boyd. "Was it worth it, son? You went through a lot of pain for nothing."

Boyd hung his head, said nothing.

"You let them beat you up pretty bad for no reason at all. I'm not going to let you out of here, and if these two shysters don't get out of my sight, I may have them arrested for any number of legal violations." To Ramsey, McBain said, "Let's get Doc over here to look at Boyd." To Stoddard and Coleman, he said, "And you two get out of my sight."

The lawyers started to bluster and splutter some argument, but McBain, with the wrath of an Old Testament prophet, raised his right arm and pointed to the front door. "Out!" he said.

Glancing back miserably at John Boyd, they left. After failing so badly in their jobs, they would undoubtedly have to face the anger of George Boyd himself.

Ramsey closed up the cell again.

Judge McBain, showing an unexpected streak of kindness, looked into Boyd's cell and said, "I'm sorry you're in so much pain, son. You shouldn't have let those two hacks talk you into it."

And with that, McBain led the way to the front office again.

Ramsey was once more thankful for the warm sunlight and the good smells of pipe tobacco and coffee.

Judge McBain shook his head. "Well, now that they've tried and failed at that, the only option left to them is violence. I take it you've met the gunslinger they hired, Robson?"

Ramsey nodded. "A couple times, as a matter of fact."

"The thing I don't understand," McBain said, "is why Robson didn't bring more men. No matter how tough those four are, the odds are that we can beat them."

Quinn spoke up, looking at Ramsey. "That's why I came back, Matt."

"Oh?"

"I was about halfway home when I saw this big cloud of dust to the west. I thought I'd see what it was."

Ramsey knew what Quinn was about to say.

"It was George Boyd and about twenty men. They're on the edge of town now, waiting."

Judge McBain shook his head. "George must have known his other plans wouldn't work out. Robson didn't scare you into letting John go—and the lawyers couldn't trick me into letting him go—so now Boyd's going to raze the town. That's the only thing left." He squinted up at the clock. "We've got nine hours before that train gets here. I wonder if we're going to make it."

Ramsey wished he could have given the judge a positive answer. But with twenty gunnies waiting on the edge of town, the odds had suddenly shifted mightily in favor of George Boyd, especially since nobody in town seemed willing to fight him.

Now Ramsey himself glanced up at the clock.

Nine hours.

Ramsey had to wonder how many of them would still be alive by the time the train rolled into the depot.

CHAPTER
★5★

1

George Boyd's men sat on a grassy plain that fell away to a creek and some timber. Many of the men were down at water's edge now refreshing their horses. It had been a long and tiring ride from the Box GB, and they knew that many long hours awaited them yet. Boyd had confided that thus far neither of his plans had worked—both his lawyers and his hired guns had failed to free his son—and now it was going to be up to his men, even though they were wranglers and not gunnies at all. There was a difference between a man who liked to raise hell at the end of a dusty, relentless cattle drive and one who killed people for hire. The wranglers had been talking about this among themselves the past few days. They were worried that George Boyd was going to force them to become the kind of men they did not want to be.

The foreman's name was Albert Conroy, and he had just finished explaining all this to Boyd.

"By God, I pay them to be my employees, and they'd damned well better do what I tell them to," Boyd snapped.

Conroy was a squat, gray-haired man whose skin had long ago turned the texture of saddle leather. Somber gray eyes stared at Boyd as he said, "I just want you to understand that up front, George. Some of the boys have serious reservations about all this."

The men stood in the copse of scrub oak, on a hill above where the men had made day camp. From up here the town of Congreve looked new and clean and prosperous, black church spires seeming to touch the blue sky itself.

Boyd said, "I mean to get my son out, Conroy, no matter what."

"I know you do, George, it's just that the boys—"

"The boys will do what I tell them!" Boyd snapped. A tall, lean man in a business suit and a white Stetson, he was imposing, especially when he was angry.

Conroy eyed him levelly. "They may not be willing to kill anybody for you, George. You've got to understand that."

Having said his piece, Conroy went back down the hill to his wranglers.

George Boyd stayed behind, smoking his pipe and looking over Congreve once again.

Twenty years ago, this had been nothing more than timber. Indians ruled the land. The few white settlers who came here quickly moved on to better lands, or what they thought were better lands, anyway. There was dust and heat in the hot months and ice and snow in the cold months. And there were rattlesnakes and cholera and Indian raids and a band of French outlaws far more treacherous than any red man had ever been. This was what George Boyd had found here. But instead of leaving, he'd decided to impose himself on it. He first cleared the land and then he brought beeves up from Texas and then he started building the town. He wanted a place for his family to be schooled and attend church and have city things to do when the time for relaxation came. Neither his first wife nor his second survived long enough to see his accomplishments but neither had been foolish enough to doubt him. They knew he'd succeed and succeed he did.

His had been the sort of western storybook life the papers back East loved to print—except for one thing. The youngest of his three children, and the only boy, had proved to have some real problems growing up. Constant trouble followed the boy around like a pet he couldn't get rid of. George Boyd blamed himself. He should have married a third time so that the boy would have had a real family life instead of the harsh environment he'd been raised up in. The boy was everything you'd want in a man—tough, purposeful, proud—but none of these attributes was tempered with kindness or perspective. He was selfish, cold and hostile. George had had hopes that the Sayles girl would show him the ways of a woman so that the boy might learn patience and kindness. But before he could change in any significant way, the boy got drunk and killed the girl in a fit of unwarranted jealousy. . . .

As he stared at the town now, George Boyd tried to imagine it in flames against the prairie night, everything his vision and cunning and resources had helped build.

Because maybe it would come to that.

Maybe that was the only way he was going to get John out of jail before the train took the boy off to the state capital for a trial and then for hanging.

But he was willing to do it, George Boyd was. Because blood kin was more important than the well-being of a town.

Especially an ungrateful town that would not peacefully turn the boy over.

He knocked his pipe out against the heel of his Texas boot and set off to town for one last try at making this lawman Matt Ramsey come to his senses.

2

"I guess I'll take that one."

"Yessir, Mr. Peck."

"And a couple boxes of those shells there."

"Sure thing, Mr. Peck."

"And while you're at it, may as well throw in a .45."

The general store clerk grinned. "You must be going to help that Ramsey fella. All this stuff, I mean. The Winchester and the shells and the .45—"

Thomas Peck winked at Sayles. "That's just what I've got in mind, Mr. Dobbs. Helping Ramsey, that is."

The clerk, starting to write everything down on a pad, shook his head. "From what I hear about those twenty men on the edge of town, that Ramsey's gonna need all the help he can get."

Peck looked at the clerk and frowned. "You mean you merchants won't be helping Ramsey?"

The clerk flushed. "We're not fighters, Mr. Peck. We're businessmen. That's why we hire our lawmen. So they can take care of things like this for us."

Peck gestured broadly around the store. It was a bountifully packed place, containing everything from cans of soup to corsets and sawn lumber to pink and green and red jelly beans. "You know what this place will look like after they get done with it."

GUNDOWN

The clerk gulped. "I know, Mr. Peck."

"But you're still not willing to pick up a rifle and defend it?"

"I've got six children, Mr. Peck."

Peck only shook his head. "Ring it up, and let me get out of here."

He was disgusted.

On the street, Sayles said, "I can't believe the cowards in this town."

Now that it was the middle of the afternoon, wagon traffic was slower. Women walked by with heavy grocery boxes. Noises from saloons were louder, more desperate. Miners drifting down from the hills were tired and dirty and obviously didn't want to worry about a bunch of gunnies hellbent on taking back some punk kid who should have been shot a long time ago.

"You thirsty?" Peck said.

"I sure would admit to that."

"Why don't we have ourselves some beer, then?"

Sayles nodded. "Don't think so much about her then."

"Pardon?"

"Amanda. When I'm drinking, I don't think so much about her."

Peck's face was suddenly so hard it looked like a map. "This is the God's truth, Mr. Sayles. There was not a moment I didn't think of her when she was alive, and there won't be a moment even now that she's dead. You have no idea how much I loved your daughter, Mr. Sayles."

Instead of being impressed, Sayles wondered if there wasn't something maybe a little wrong with love like that. Something strange . . .

"Let's go have those beers," Sayles said.

• • •

"I don't need to tell you how much I loved her," Thomas Peck said after they had hoisted their second beer.

"No, you don't, son."

"Or the plans I had for us."

"I know, son."

"Or the family I planned."

Robert Sayles nodded solemnly.

"I didn't do everything right, and I admit it," Peck said.

Sayles started to shrug, but Peck went on, almost as if the older man weren't standing right beside him at the bar. "I don't think she ever understood how much I loved her."

Neutrally as he could, Sayles said, "Maybe not, son."

"I don't think she ever understood how pure my love for her was. And how it would have lasted forever."

Now Sayles definitely had the impression that Thomas Peck was talking to himself.

Peck sipped his beer, continued to stare into the mirror behind the bar. "When I heard that she was dead—"

Sayles heard a sob catch in the other man's throat.

"You really did love her, didn't you?"

"That I did, Mr. Sayles. That I did."

But comforting as Thomas Peck's words should have been now, there was something . . . strange about them.

As if his love for Amanda had been . . . too much . . . or even maybe . . . twisted in some way.

He looked over at Peck, who now had his hand on the holster of his .45. Peck looked angry.

Uncomfortable, Sayles said, "I forget—you went to school with John Boyd, didn't you?"

"We all went to school together. Amanda, John and me. I thought he was my friend and then—" He shook his head and made a bitter face. "And then he took my woman from me."

Sayles started to say that Amanda had been frightened of Peck—of his incredibly jealous rages—but thought the better of it.

This man, after all, was the only real friend Sayles had in the whole town of Congreve.

"You're a true friend, Thomas," Sayles said, feeling lonely and a little beered up now.

Peck offered one of his rare smiles. "And you're a true friend to me, too. Yes, indeed."

He pulled Sayles closer and gave him a little hug. Sayles had never known how strong Peck was.

It was a wonder that the time Peck and John Boyd had got into a fistfight outside of the Sayles shack . . . it was a wonder that Peck hadn't killed Boyd.

Sayles glanced up at Peck in a new way, now. Sure, Thomas Peck was a good friend, but given the spooky way he talked about Amanda and the cold-blooded way he was planning Boyd's death . . . well, there was definitely something frightening about Peck, too.

Very frightening.

3

Matt Ramsey said, "I want you to tell me about the other night."

John Boyd, lying on his back on the cell cot, said, "Why?"

"I'm just interested in all—"

Boyd frowned. "In all the dirty details."

"No, just in how it happened."

Boyd sighed. "Truth is, I don't remember much."

Long late afternoon shadows fell across Boyd's face as he spoke. Outside the temperature had dropped several degrees. In the cells, it was cool enough for blankets now. If Boyd minded the chill, he didn't let on.

"Why'd you get so mad at her?" Ramsey said.

Boyd stared into space. "She was going to break it off."

"She found somebody else?"

Boyd shook his head. His dark gaze was sad. "No, my drinking. 'Carousing,' she always called it."

"She'd threatened to do this before?"

"Sure. A lot of times."

"But you never struck her before?"

Boyd sat up on the cot. From his pocket he took the makings and started to roll himself a cigarette. "I know my reputation, Ramsey. But there's nobody—no matter how much he hates me—who'll say that I hit women."

"Then why did you hit her?"

Boyd shook his head, stuck the cigarette in his mouth. "Like I say, I don't remember doing it."

"Or strangling her?"

Boyd squeezed his eyes shut. "I . . . don't remember that, either."

Ramsey paused a long time before speaking again. "You confessed the other night."

"I know."

"Are you taking your confession back?"

Boyd looked at him. He looked young and scared. "No, I don't guess I am."

"Then you should stand trial."

Boyd smiled sadly. "That's why you came in here, wasn't it?"

"I wanted to see what you remembered from the other night. Sam Curry was a sick man when he was questioning you. I just thought there might have been something he'd overlooked."

Boyd's smile stayed on his face. "And you wouldn't mind if I'd talk to my old man, either, would you?" Every few minutes or so he grimaced from the beating the lawyer had given him.

"I'd be appreciative. There's no reason for this town to be torn apart."

Boyd shook his head. "You don't know my dad."

"He's got twenty men camped on the edge of town."

Boyd whistled. "I knew he had Robson here."

"You know Robson?"

"Sure. Everybody in these parts does." He grinned like a kid. "He's a bad man. Faster with a gun than anybody I ever saw. So are his men." Boyd nodded to Ramsey's gun belt. "Are you fast, Ramsey?"

"Not as fast as I'd like."

"Then I'd stay away from Robson if I was you."

Ramsey said, "You could stop it all."

"I suppose I could."

"I could go get your father for you."

Boyd said, "You ever see a man hanged?"

"Several times. In the war."

"I only did once. But I still have nightmares about it."

"If your lawyer was smart, he'd plead you second degree and you wouldn't have to worry about a hanging."

"You know how long judges and juries in this territory have been waiting to get their hands on somebody with the last name of Boyd. My father may be powerful, but I never forget that he's also got a lot of enemies. A lot of them, Ramsey, and some of them are bound to show up on that jury. One look at me and—" He slowly shook his head and exhaled blue smoke in the chill shadows. "I'm afraid

I can't help you, Ramsey. My dad came here to take me home, and that's just where I plan to go—home."

"You won't be there for long. He'll have to get you to the border and Mexico."

Boyd snorted. "You may find this hard to believe, Ramsey, but living out my days next to a peaceful blue sea sounds a lot better to me than dangling from the end of a rope." His ribs started hurting again, and he grimaced and sucked in air fast and swore under his breath.

"Your friend Stoddard got a little carried away," Ramsey said.

Boyd looked up at him and frowned.

Ramsey was just about to say good-bye when the door to the cell opened and Deputy Quinn said, "You'd better come fast, Ramsey. One of Robson's men picked a fight with a town man and he's about ready to shoot him down."

Ramsey looked at Boyd. All the kid could think to do was drop his eyes.

"Come on," Ramsey said to Quinn.

Once again a crowd had gathered, bigger than the earlier one because the mines had let out.

In the middle of the street, over by the stone schoolhouse, two men faced each other. One was the man with the scarred face, one of Robson's gunnies. The other was a skinny, gangly kid of maybe twenty who wore the faded britches and faded workshirt of a farm boy. He wore black boots that came up to his knees.

Robson's gunny said, "Now, kid, I'm givin' you one last chance. You pick up that gun or I'm gonna draw down on you."

A silver Colt lay in the dust at the kid's feet.

Five feet to his right sat a wagon. A young girl with a bonnet sat up there looking terrified. Likely this was the kid's young sister or wife.

Robson and the other gunnies were nowhere to be seen. The gunnie had probably started this little war by himself. Gunnies got bored quickly.

"You pick it up now, hear?" the gunnie said. "So nobody can say it wasn't a fair fight."

The kid looked up to the girl in the wagon. He gulped. He was as scared as she was.

Ramsey stepped in front of the kid. The crowd moved back.

"Get up on the wagon, kid, and drive out of here," Ramsey said.

The gunnie said, "He tried to run me over, Sheriff."

"Ain't true!" the kid screeched. "Ain't true! He got in front of us when m'wife and me was comin' down the street."

"Get in the wagon and get out of here," Ramsey said again. "You hear me?"

"Yessir."

The gunnie drew so fast Ramsey scarcely saw him do it. The gunnie fired two dust-raising shots at the kid's feet.

"This fight is between me'n him," the gunnie said.

The kid froze, not knowing what to do.

"Put the gun away," Ramsey said.

The gunnie laughed. "And I suppose you're going to make me?"

"Could be. Now put it away before we have real trouble here."

"Like I said, Ramsey, this fight's between the kid and me."

Ramsey waved to the kid to finish getting up into the

wagon. The kid looked first at the gunnie and then back to Ramsey. He took one more step.

The gunny turned and started to fire.

Ramsey's .45 came out flaming. He put a big hole, a big puddle, right in the gunny's left shoulder.

The gunny cried out and went over backward in the late afternoon shadows and dust.

The air smelled of gunsmoke. The echoes of gunfire bounced off the front of the school.

The crowd made noises of excitement and fear. Nothing was quite as much fun as seeing another man gunned down—when you were involved only as a spectator, that is—and nothing brought up quite so much fear, either, because it could always be you taking the bullet and falling into the dust.

Ramsey went over to the gunny. The man's right hand was groping toward his own weapon.

Ramsey kicked the weapon away.

"You'd better get over and see the doc," Ramsey said. "That's a pretty bad wound."

"You son of a bitch," the gunny said, the scar along his jawline looking even more prominent now. "Robson ain't going to like this."

"Robson knows where to find me," Ramsey said.

Then he turned to the people. "It's getting on toward dinnertime now. You folks go on home."

"You're a real fast draw!" one man said enthusiastically. He sounded as if he were at a circus.

"Go on, now," Ramsey said.

He almost gave them a little speech about the type of people who wanted to stand around and see two men shoot at each other . . . but who wouldn't pick up guns of their own and fight to save their hometown.

GUNDOWN

Most of the crowd started to walk away at his orders. Except for one man. He came up to Ramsey with the purposeful stride of a proud and confident man.

"I wanted to see what I was up against. I have to say I was impressed."

"Beg pardon?" Ramsey said to the man.

"I heard Sam got sick and you took over. I wondered what mettle of man you were. I just found out."

"I see."

"That gunny's a tough son of a bitch. You handled him with no problem."

"Maybe I got lucky."

The man snorted. "Oh, it was a lot more than luck. You're faster on the draw and you've got a much steadier hand than that gunny. And that's saying something."

"Mind if I ask your name, mister?" Ramsey said. But he already had a good idea of who he was talking to.

"Boyd," the man said. "George Boyd."

Ramsey didn't give him the satisfaction of looking surprised. He just said, "That's what I figured."

"Let's go over to the jail and talk some," George Boyd said. "We need to talk."

4

Sada Tomlin didn't wake up till late afternoon. The first thing she did was reach across to the nightstand for the bottle of whiskey she kept for herself and her customers. Maude Lane, the fat woman who ran this house, didn't approve of Sada's "excessive drinking," as she always called it, but Sada was her most popular girl, so there was little Maude could do about it. All the other "girls" were actually well-worn middle-aged ladies whom Maude's customers complained about constantly. Women who lacked teeth and even a semblance of breeding did not inspire great lust on the part of drovers and miners.

Sada was different, though. A very slight, pretty twenty-year-old who had run away from some legal trouble in St. Louis—she'd stood by while her boyfriend had cut a man's throat just before taking his money—she'd come to Congreve three years ago and had immediately become the most popular girl in Maude's "crib."

Sada never let Maude forget this, either. Sada had steak for dinner, a Negro woman to clean her room every day, and a clothing allowance. Sada loved the feel of silk against her tawny skin, and the look of ribbons in her tumbling dark hair.

In order to acquire all these privileges, Sada had to endure the foolishness and mendacity of men—men of all ages, sizes and inclinations. There were the laughable men who paid to be with her even though they couldn't get erections; there were the pathetic men who couldn't last more than a minute or two once they got inside her; and there were the dangerous men who liked violence far more than they liked sex.

She'd been with such a man a few nights earlier, and she was still hurting from the punches he'd driven into her face and ribs. It had happened very quickly, before she could much more than roll away from his blows, and then when it was over, he'd sat—a big, brooding man—in the moonlit corner of her room, chest heaving, glaring down at his fists as if he were trying to will them out of existence . . .

"I'm sorry," he'd said.

She lay on the bed, touching her wounds carefully. She said nothing.

"Did you hear me?" he said.

"Yes."
"Well, do you believe me?"
"That you're sorry?"
"Yes."
"I guess so."
"Something just comes over me."

At such times she always thought of running away, just as she'd run away from St. Louis.

It seemed each year, the beatings got worse and worse. She'd heard stories of women who'd been bludgeoned to death then buried out in the country so the law couldn't find the bodies and ask questions.

She knew that eventually this would happen to her.

The wrong night.

The wrong man.

One who wouldn't be satisfied with just extracting a little pain and a few cries from her.

One who'd settle for nothing less than her death.

"I'd be happy to buy you a new hat tomorrow," the man said.

He was strange, even by the standards of violent men. Most of them never apologized. They just seemed to assume that the greenbacks they'd given Maude were adequate compensation for beating the hell out of her girls.

But this man was . . . different. And disturbingly so. His remorse was so all-consuming that it made her uncomfortable.

He stood up and put on his hat and said, "I'd better be going now."

She said nothing.

"I was serious about buying you that hat."

She said nothing.

He made his way to the door, stared back at her through the

shadows. The whole house had come alive with noise in their silence—the player piano, the laughter of drunken women, the harsh jocularity of boy-men having themselves a good illicit time away from dutiful and deadeningly dull wives.

"You sure about that hat?"

Said nothing, again. Stared at the shadows playing on the wall. Sick of herself. Sick of her life. In pain.

And then, quietly, he left, closing the door softly behind him.

Later, unable to handle any more men this evening, she went down the hall to the washroom and waited out a drover who was puking up his dinner and his drinks. Then she cleaned herself up and decided to go for a walk.

And that was how she saw it all.

She was walking out by the small riverside park when she heard the arguing voices.

There near the store she saw them, like two shadows they were, the Boyd boy and his beautiful but somewhat priggish girlfriend, Amanda Sayles.

Sada was fascinated by their argument. She slipped into the darkness of timber and listened.

The Boyd boy was angry over something Amanda said— Sada didn't understand what—and he was pacing around in furious circles.

Suddenly, he lashed out, striking her—

Amanda fell in a heap to the ground.

For a long time there were just the noises of the night. The rushing river. Barking dogs. The faint saloon music blocks away.

John Boyd knelt next to Amanda then.

Picked up her hand. Checked for a pulse.

Sada could feel his panic, even from here.

He jumped to his feet and started stumbling drunkenly

away, making little mewling wounded-animal sounds as he moved.

Obviously, he was under the impression he'd killed her.

Obviously, he was trying to get away.

Sada was about to step from the shadows to go and see if she could help the girl when she saw Amanda abruptly stand up.

The young woman looked at first as if she'd fall back down, but then she righted herself, began taking deep breaths and drew herself up straight.

Clearly, she was fine. Rattled, perhaps, probably very afraid, as well . . . but physically she was in good shape.

And that's when the man appeared.

The same man who'd been in Sada's room earlier in the evening. The rough but apologetic one.

He said nothing to Amanda.

Just walked over to her and slapped her hard across the mouth.

Then his hands were on her throat, and he was choking her, and this time when Amanda sank to the ground, Sada knew that she was dead.

Amanda lay in the moonlit grass, silent.

The man stood over her, gasping as he had with Sada.

Already, he was starting to cry. He knew he'd killed her. His remorse was almost palpable.

Sada made a noise, too, a tiny whimper.

The man's head snapped up, eyes frantically searching the darkness.

"Is somebody there?" he called.

She clung to the tree, her body covered with icy sweat.

"Is somebody there?" he called again.

Her breathing pounded in her ears.

She heard his footsteps in the grass coming closer, closer.

"I said, is somebody there?" he repeated.

He sounded angry now.

She thought of his big fists and trembled. He was not a heavy man, but he was tall and had inordinate strength.

And then she bolted.

She knew if she clung to the tree any longer, he'd find her and kill her.

So she ran, slipping, through the dewy grass. Once, she banged her head against a tree. For a horrible moment, she felt as if she might pass out . . .

But she kept running, running. She wanted to tear her skirt away so she could run even faster.

And he was somewhere behind her.

Drawing closer, closer.

Finally, her feet reached the hard-packed dirt of a street. A lantern glowed several feet ahead.

For the first time, she allowed herself the luxury of turning around and looking behind her.

He stood, out of breath, on the edge of the park. She could see his crazed eyes glowing in the darkness.

He'd come so close—

She hurried on back to Maude's.

The place was packed with revelers. She went straight to her room, closed the door.

She sat up all night in a chair, a .45 packed solidly in her hand.

The man didn't come.

Around dawn, light pearl-gray against the window, she fell into a troubled sleep.

"Sleepin' kind of late, ain't you?"

Maude enjoyed picking on Sada. She obviously resented the young woman her looks, her charms.

Sada shrugged and poured herself a cup of coffee. They were in the kitchen. The shadows of late afternoon made it cool, almost chill.

Sada doused some whiskey into her coffee.

"Little early for that, ain't it?" Maude said.

Sada smiled. "Never too early, far as I'm concerned."

"You won't keep your looks that way, I'll tell you that." Maude looked her over. "You dressed to go out someplace?"

Sada nodded. "Got an appointment."

"Oh?"

"Won't take long."

"Who's your appointment with?"

"Thought you weren't going to ask me any more questions like that," Sada said. Last week the two women had gotten into an argument about the way Maude was always playing mother hen and asking for answers that were none of her business.

Maude shook her head. "Try to be friendly and look what I get."

Sada sipped her coffee. Actually, now that the time was here, she was nervous.

Since waking up this afternoon, she'd figured out how she was going to get away from Maude's for good and have enough money to start life over in Chicago or someplace fancy like that.

Sada had a secret to sell.

And she planned to sell it to the highest bidder.

5

Ramsey handed George Boyd a cup of coffee. "You were saying, Mr. Boyd?"

"I was saying that I don't want trouble any more than you do."

Ramsey sipped at his own coffee. "Then you'll be willing to see your son put on that train tonight."

Boyd shook his head. "If I was anybody else, Ramsey, I'd be willing to let him stand trial. But my son—well, I've got a lot of enemies in this territory. You know that and I know that. Everybody who's ever wanted to pay me back will be jumping on my son. Especially the people up in the capital."

"Your son confessed to killing a girl."

Boyd watched Ramsey carefully. After a pause, he said, "Have you ever considered the fact that maybe the killing was accidental?"

"Maybe it was. That'll be for the jury to decide."

"As I said, I'd be willing to let him take his chances with an impartial jury but—"

Boyd shook his head again. He looked older and less powerful now—whipped, Ramsey supposed, by all the tension. While Boyd was a cattle baron used to getting his way, he'd rarely had to depend on pure force to get it. This would be a new and wearing approach for him—to threaten violence against the very town that he'd built.

Boyd said, "I know how the town leaders feel about what you're doing."

"If you're talking about Stufflebeam, so do I."

"It'd be easier if you'd just hand John over."

"I know it would be easier, Mr. Boyd. But it wouldn't be right."

Boyd sighed. "Despite everything you've heard about him, John isn't a bad kid. It was the way he was raised—and that was my fault."

Ramsey sensed a deep sorrow and remorse in the man.

He also sensed the weariness again.

"He likes his whiskey and he likes his fistfights, Ramsey Boyd said. "But he's a long way from being a killer."

"How do you explain the dead girl, then?"

Boyd shrugged. "I came to see him the morning Sam put him in jail. John doesn't remember much of what happened. He could have hit her and—"

"Strangulation isn't accidental, I'm afraid. When you strangle somebody, you mean to do it."

"But if he was drunk—"

"Again, Mr. Boyd, those are things a jury will have to take into account."

Boyd stood up. He walked over to the window and looked out at the street. Lanterns had just come on in the soft dusk. "It took me a long time to build this place," he said almost wistfully.

"That's what I hear."

Boyd snorted. "At first nobody thought I could do it. According to the bankers, I didn't have enough money, I didn't have enough land, I didn't have enough brains." Boyd was mocking all his old enemies. "But by God, I showed them, Ramsey. I built this town into a showcase."

Boyd turned back from the window. "And I don't want to tear it down. That would break my heart, if you can understand that."

"Sure."

"So I'm asking you to help me, Ramsey. I know that Robson tried to buy you off and that didn't work—and I made a mistake approaching you that way. You're an ethical man. Most of the time, so am I, believe it or not."

"I'm sure you are."

"So I won't try to bribe you. I'll just appeal to your reason. You don't want to see this town torn apart, do you?"

"No, I don't."

"It's not your town, anyway, Ramsey. You were just passing through to say hello to an old friend of yours."

"That's Stufflebeam's argument."

"What is?"

"That since it's not my town, I should just hand John over."

"It makes sense, when you think about it."

"The law's the law whether this is my town or not," Ramsey said.

Boyd stared at him. "Is there anything you want from this life, Ramsey?"

"Peace of mind. All the time I was in the war, that's all I could think of. I just wanted peace of mind. And to be left alone."

Boyd stared at him. "Not money?"

"No."

"I'd double what Robson offered."

Ramsey shook his head, drained his coffee.

"I've got some nice land, Ramsey. With some nice beeves. You could be a gentleman cattleman."

"No, thanks."

"You're going to turn him over, then?"

"Yes, I am, Mr. Boyd. I'm sorry that you're going through all this. You're his father and you love him. But I've still got to hand him over. I don't have much choice in the matter."

"You know what's going to happen next, don't you?"

Ramsey shrugged. "I suppose Robson and his men will get busy."

"And the men I've got camped on the edge of town."

Ramsey dropped his eyes, shook his head. "I wish you'd reconsider." He looked up at Boyd. "Even if you manage to free him, Mr. Boyd, he'll still be a wanted fugitive."

"There's always Mexico."

"If you think he could be happy there."

"He'd be a damn sight happier than getting a noose around his neck." Boyd sighed. "I'd like to see him."

"Sure. But I'm going to have to ask you to leave your gun out here."

"All right."

"And then I'll have to search you for any other guns."

"I'm not a common criminal."

"I know that, Mr. Boyd. But you're the boy's father and right now you're a pretty desperate man."

The weariness returned to Boyd's gaze.

He sighed again and held his arms out as Ramsey began to search him.

Morty Boyd had spent the past four hours trying to gather up a group of men who would fight his uncle George Boyd if necessary. Thus far, he hadn't recruited a single man. The most common excuse offered was "I have a family, Morty; you don't." Morty was still a bachelor.

Now, as dusk tainted the sky a curious but beautiful salmon color, and as a quarter moon appeared above the foothills, Morty bought himself a bucket of beer from one of the saloons and took it back to the livery stable.

Not everybody in Congreve approved of how Morty treated his black stable "boy" Eddie. Basically he treated him the way he would a white employee.

Now, for instance, Eddie's work done for the day, Morty invited him to share the bucket of beer. Some said it wasn't right to drink with a colored. Morty didn't much give a damn what the town people thought.

"How'd it go this afternoon?" Eddie asked as they seated themselves on a log near the rope corral. Some of the horses were settling in for the night.

"Didn't get a single person."

"Didn't figure you would, I guess."

"My uncle's got everybody scared. Just the way he had my father scared." Morty Boyd tried never to think of his father—a cowering, terrified figure who'd done anything his older brother George asked him to until the day he dropped dead from a disease nobody knew he had, including himself. Not even Morty's mother had any dignity or self-respect, always running to George for money or help of some other kind. Not Morty. He'd done it all on his own, and that included beating up his spoiled-brat cousin John Boyd. Morty had no doubts that John had killed Amanda Sayles. At last, the law was catching up to the George Boyd family.

"I went and did something this afternoon, Morty."

"Did what?"

"Got me a rifle."

"What?"

"Over to the general store. Lem didn't want to sell it to me seeing I'm colored and all, but he finally gave in."

"Eddie, you're too old to—"

"Somebody's got to help you and Sheriff Ramsey."

Morty laughed and clapped Eddie on the back. "Now isn't that something for you?"

"Beg pardon?"

"All these proud white people in this town—and you're the only one who's willing to stand up to my uncle."

Now Eddie laughed, too. "I guess it is kind of crazy."

Morty sombered quickly. "It's going to be bad, Eddie."

GUNDOWN

"I know."

"Bloody."

"I know."

"And with Robson and his gunnies backing him up—"

Eddie sighed. "You scared?"

"Yup. You?"

Eddie nodded. "Real scared. But I'm gettin' my rifle anyway."

Morty poured them some more beer. "Why don't we finish this up, then I'll go give Ramsey the bad news that you and I are the only townspeople who'll stand behind him."

They sat there in the dusk, finishing the beer. It was so peaceful, the stars out now, the horses gentling down for the night.

But it wouldn't be peaceful for long, and they knew it.

Just after the door closed behind him, George Boyd stood in the shadows of the jail, looking at his son in the far cell. The boy was facing away, hunched over in a fetal position.

Ramsey had given George a lantern. George held it high now, glancing around the gloomy jail. Everything smelled damp, mildewed.

George was bombarded with memories of the boy at different ages. As usual, he felt remorse for how the boy had been raised—if his mother had lived, surely the boy would have turned out differently.

George went up to John's cell. "You asleep?"

Long pause. Back still to George. "No."

John had a way of blaming his father for everything. That's why he was so sullen now. Somehow, in his mind, this was all his father's fault.

"That wasn't my idea, to beat you up. Stoddard and Coleman talked me into it."

"I really enjoyed it," John said. "It felt really good."

"No reason to be sarcastic."

"No reason at all. Just because I'm going to be hanged."

"Quit talking like that."

"It's the truth."

"The hell it is and you know it."

"Six hours till that train pulls in."

"A lot can happen in six hours."

John quit talking then, started to sit up. He made low grunts of pain.

George looked away. He hated to see his son this way.

John sat on the edge of the couch and said, "You won't be able to pull this one off."

"I'll level this town if I have to."

"That's just what you'll need to do."

George said, "You shouldn't have confessed."

"I killed her, didn't I?"

"You were drunk. Who knows what happened? Maybe it was an accident."

John grinned. "Some accident. Strangulation."

"Maybe she made you mad."

"You really think that was an excuse to kill her?"

"You sound like you want them to hang you."

John glanced up. He looked sadder than George had ever seen him. "Maybe I do. Maybe that's exactly what I want."

"Don't talk foolish."

"What the hell good am I to anybody, anyway? That's why Amanda wanted to be done with me. Because I was a spoiled child, according to her, and that's all I'd ever be."

"She didn't know how rough you had it. Growing up, I mean."

The mirthless smile returned to John's face. "People

around here have a hard time thinking of me as disadvantaged. I'm your son, after all."

George said again, "I'm getting you out of here."

"How?"

"I've got twenty men on the edge of town."

"And Robson's still here?"

"Yes."

John shook his head. "Good old Robson. How he loves to kill people."

"He kills only when necessary."

"Well, he sure finds a lot of necessaries, then."

"I'd think you'd be grateful to him. He's pulled you out of some tough scrapes before. That time in Cheyenne when they caught you cheating at cards—"

"He shot the guy in the back. And he didn't need to shoot him at all. I'd already made an agreement with the guy to pay back the money and walk away clean."

"Well, Robson got you out, didn't he?"

John shook his head again. He lay back down on the couch. His face was tight from pain. "You remember that hanging you took me to?"

"That was a long time ago."

"I still have nightmares about it."

"You were too young. I shouldn't have taken you."

"That's what I'm going to look like soon enough. The way he did there. Dangling." He paused. "I'm scared."

"I know."

"You've got to get me out of here, Dad."

"I know. And I will."

"They really want to hang me."

"No, son, they want to hang me, but the only way they can get to me is through you."

"Tell Robson to do what he needs to."

"That's exactly what I'll tell him."

"And hurry. That train's coming soon."

"I'll go talk to Robson right now."

Then George heard a sound he hadn't heard in long years. John turned over on his cot and started crying.

George hefted the lantern in his hand and went back to the front of the jail.

6

There was a back way up the hotel and Sada was familiar with it. On occasion, she came here to do her work. On these occasions men—usually rich cattlemen—paid Maude two or three times the going rate to have Sada come to their rooms.

Now Sada was here on a mission of her own.

On the third floor, she paused on the stairs, opened the fire door and went inside.

The hallway smelled of smoke from cigars and the guttering lamps.

She went down to the center of the hall, knocked.

No answer.

She knocked again.

This time she heard bedsprings squeak. A body got up from the bed, made those small noises people always do on waking, then set feet to floor and walked over and opened the door.

He stood there staring at her. Right now he had no idea who she was. He had his trousers on and a summer undershirt.

"You don't remember me, do you?"

He was still half-asleep. "No, I—"

GUNDOWN 87

"That's not very flattering," she said coyly.

"Oh. Wait. The other night."

"Now that's more like it," she smiled. "The other night."

"You and I—"

"Yes. You and I."

"What're you doing here?"

"Thought we could have a little talk."

"I'm sorry but I don't have time for—"

"No. I meant a talk. Not—the other thing."

"Talk about what?"

Her sweeping arm indicated the hallway. "I don't think you'd want anyone to see me standing out here."

"But—"

"So why don't I just come in?"

And she did.

Pushed right past him into the room.

Flocked wallpaper and heavy mahogany furnishings lent the small room a rich look. She'd never be able to afford a room like this.

She closed the door.

"Did you bring a lot of cash with you to town?"

"I beg your pardon."

"Cash. Greenbacks. Did you bring a lot of them with you."

He looked irritated. "Exactly what the hell are you getting at?"

She smiled sweetly. "After you left the other night, I went for a walk."

"Not to be rude, but I don't especially give a damn what you did or didn't do the other night."

"I walked over by the river."

For the first time, fear showed in his eyes. She felt enormous satisfaction at this first glimpse of his apprehension.

"I saw Amanda Sayles and John Boyd."

"Why tell me this?"

"Because after John left, I also saw somebody else."

Now he stood in the middle of the room, glaring at her in the dim lamplight.

"I saw you."

"I don't know what you're talking about."

"I saw you. You're the one who killed her."

"I wasn't anywhere near the river that night."

"Oh yes you were, and unless you pay me a lot of money, I'm going to tell George Boyd just exactly what I saw."

Thomas Peck seemed to loom over her suddenly, and for the first time she was struck by the cold oddness of this man. She sensed how dangerous he could be.

She backed up a little, toward the door.

"I want the money now," she said, trying to keep the air of threat in her tone.

"I want you out of here."

"You killed her."

"And I want you out of here now."

"You killed her, and I'm going to tell George Boyd."

"You tell George Boyd whatever you want. He's not going to listen to some whore."

"He'll give me money, and then they'll hang you instead."

He slapped her then.

Just once but so hard that she sank to her knees and started whimpering.

"You didn't see anything the other night," he said.

She stumbled back toward the bed.

He came after her. "Do you hear me?" he said. "You didn't see anything the other night?"

He slapped her hard again, and then he grabbed the front of her dress and tore it straight down.

GUNDOWN

Her small, well-formed breasts bobbed free. He took one of them in his hand and twisted it.

As she tried to scream, he clamped his hand over her mouth and pushed her back onto the bed.

Over the next few minutes, she thought of how people would laugh when they heard her tell somebody that she'd been raped.

A whore. Raped.

That would be good for a laugh.

All the time he was inside her, pumping away, he kept his hand tight over her mouth.

By now, of course, she realized that she'd made a terrible mistake coming here.

She should have known that any man who could strangle a woman in cold blood . . .

When he was finished with her, he backed out and rolled off her. He was careful to keep his hand over her mouth. He knew she'd scream.

He was trying to figure out what to do. His plans had been so easy. Amanda would be dead for betraying him, and John Boyd would suffer the public humiliation of hanging. And—

So easy.

But now there was this little bitch. . . .

Almost without thinking, he rolled over again, moving very close to her. Her eyes were wide. She seemed to sense what was coming next.

"You really would turn me in, wouldn't you?"

She shook her head.

He laughed. She looked so pathetic now, all the venom gone from her gaze, all the mendacity from her voice.

"Oh, you wouldn't turn me over?"

She nodded.

"Oh, I had you all wrong," he said coyly. "Here I thought you were a little whore without any ethics or scruples. But I was wrong, wasn't I?"

Again, she nodded like a little girl desperately trying to please.

"You're a fine, upstanding citizen and a very good friend of mine, right?"

Once more, she nodded.

His hands found her throat so quickly, like pouncing animals.

Her face turned several different shades of color before she died.

She moved against him with her entire body, as if they were once more in the midst of sex, and he could see her trying to scream, but it did no good, of course.

She tried to scratch him, kick him, even twist her head so she could bite him.

But it was all to no avail.

Because his hands were steady and true, pushing, pushing, pushing the life from her.

Finally, she flopped beneath him uselessly. She had given up the struggle.

He no longer had to worry about her struggling. Not now.

As he rose from the bed, he felt the quick, dark remorse of the other night. He should, he knew, feel joy for vanquishing an enemy—in the end, Amanda had become an enemy—but there was just a darkness now, a hollowness he could not explain.

He shuddered then with an almost seismic convulsion as he looked at her tiny, semi-naked body on the bed.

The curious thing was that now he wondered about her as a person. What she'd really been like. What had pleased her. What had displeased her. What her dreams had been.

He had killed more than a woman here tonight. He had killed an entire history.

He went back to the bed, lifted her up, slung her over his shoulder and carried her over to the closet.

He pushed his clothes aside and set her in the rear of the small, dark room.

She would be all right here till he could come back later tonight and take her down the back way and put her in a buckboard and then get her out of town and bury her someplace in the prairie.

She didn't smell, that was the other thing.

By the time Amanda had died the other night, she'd smelled terribly.

He closed the door.

He supposed Sada didn't smell simply because different people reacted to violent death differently.

He went over and washed his hands.

He washed them so hard and so long they began to ache.

It was as if he were trying to wash off some permanent stain.

The dark hollowness of remorse filled his chest.

He tried not to think about it.

He just kept washing his hands.

7

"You know what I'm remembering?"
"What?"
"What you looked like in your first-communion dress."
"Oh."
"And you know what else I was thinking about?"
"What?"

"The time you climbed up in that haymow and got that bat caught in your hair."

"That one I'll never forget."

"I hope you'll always remember how much your mother and I loved you, Rita."

She forced a laugh. "You'll be around a long time to keep reminding me."

Sam Curry lay in bed, his head propped up on pillows Rita kept nervously fluffing every half hour or so.

A kerosene lamp lent the room a soft glow. On his nightstand, Rita had set her mother's leather-covered Bible. In Sam's big, blunt fingers was wound a black rosary.

"Remember the kitten you had? Fluffy?" he said.

"I sure do. I think about her every day."

He smiled. "You used to sleep with her."

"She'd bite my toes. I hardly got any sleep at all."

"And your horse Samuel?"

She giggled. It was a girlish sound and it was pleasant in this soft, quiet room. "I named him after you."

"And I was flattered."

"Big and strong and good and true."

"Well, I certainly thank you for all those kind words."

And then she saw it, the knitting of the eyebrows in pain, the tightening of the mouth and the locking of the jaws.

He was having troubles again.

Her heart fluttered like a wild bird in panic.

Should she summon the doctor again?

But might not summoning the doctor only increase her father's anxiety and bring on another heart attack?

She put her hand on his.

Pressed against her palm, the black rosary beads felt like loose kernels of corn.

"I remember the day you and Mother took me to the fair."

"Oh, that was a fine day, wasn't it? I remember that one, too."

"I won a nickel because I guessed that clown's weight."

"And you got sick because you ate so much candy."

He looked at her then.

Just stared at her, him in bed, her right beside him, her small hand covering his big one.

He looked as if he wanted to say something somber and serious and quite important. But then a curious smile touched his lips and shone in his blue eyes and she saw how delicate he was despite his size and his sometimes gruff manner.

"Dad—" she started to say.

And then he died.

Just then and just so, lying in the white bed like that with her tiny hand on his big one, and she started to say again "Dad—" but knew it was too late.

She didn't move.

She didn't say anything.

Just sat there next to him.

Looking and remembering.

Dad.

And then the tears came. They weren't aggrieved or harsh tears but soft and silent ones, silver on her spinster cheeks.

Dad.

She wanted to feel rage, to rail against the Boyds for bringing this on, against the town for not backing him up.

But for this long, prayerlike moment there was just a dizzying number of good memories.

Dad.

Dead.

And the world would never be the same. The footsteps on the morning stairs, coming down for breakfast. The tune he whistled every day as he shaved. The way he sat in the rocker smoking his pipe and reading his paper every night.

No more.

And now the tears came hard and harsh, and she did blame the Boyds for killing her father.

She blamed them very much.

8

Morty Boyd and his stable hand Eddie stood in the doorway. Each of them carried a rifle.

"Afraid I wasn't much good at recruiting a lot of help for you, Ramsey."

Fifteen minutes earlier Ramsey had said good-bye to George Boyd. After visiting his son in the jail cell, Boyd's eyes had watered over with tears, and there was a look of purpose and determination in his gaze. It was clear he was going to get his son out before the train came.

Now Ramsey was at one of the gun racks, checking the carbines for ammunition.

"Didn't figure you'd find much help in this town," Ramsey said.

"Stufflebeam's gone around to all the merchants and warned them about what could happen if they made George Boyd mad. Said that if George ever decided to take all his money out of the bank, the bank would be in pretty sorry shape."

Ramsey nodded to the street. "He was just here. Went in back and saw your cousin John."

For the first time sympathy shone in Morty's eyes. "Poor bastard. I know how much he loves John. He really does."

Ramsey shook his head. "In this circumstance, it just makes him all the more dangerous."

Eddie said, hoisting his rifle, "We're here, anyway. How about some of that coffee?"

"Appreciate the help, men. And the coffee's all yours."

As the two came into the office, Morty said, "Where's Quinn?"

"Home finishing dinner. I told him to take two hours."

"You think he's coming back?"

Ramsey shrugged. "I suppose. Why?"

"Most wives in this town would try to talk their husbands out of it."

In answer to his question, Deputy Quinn came striding through the door, a Winchester balanced in his hand.

"What was that you were saying?" Ramsey smiled to Morty.

"I wasn't saying anything at all," Morty said.

Eddie had just finished pouring himself a cup of coffee when the first shot shattered the glass above Ramsey's desk.

The second shot panged off the low-hanging Rochester lamp.

The third and fourth shots shattered more glass on the east-facing windows.

By now, all four men were crouched behind desks and chairs.

"Didn't take your uncle long to give Harry Robson the word to put his gunnies to work," Ramsey said.

Morty laughed. "Nobody ever accused Uncle George of dawdling."

Then Morty stood up and started firing back through one of the windows.

He must have had some luck. In the shadows across the street, a man screamed.

Gunfire from Robson's gunnies was immediate. The Rochester lamp was shot out completely. The office was in darkness. Through the shattered windows, Ramsey could see the tops of the false fronts across the street and the stars bright in the night sky beyond.

Ramsey crawled over to a chair directly beneath the east-facing window.

He eased himself up, ready to throw himself to the floor if any firing started, and took a look at the street.

He saw a man crouching down and running toward the sheriff's office.

Ramsey fired three times with the carbine.

Shots two and three lifted the man off the ground. For a long moment he hung in the air with his arms thrown back, like some sort of swimmer about to make a big dive, and then he came down hard and dead on the street.

So far, in less than five minutes, two of Robson's men had been killed.

At this rate, it wouldn't be long before George Boyd was forced to use his own men, who were waiting on the edge of town.

The next bullet came from the other side and caught Eddie directly in the face.

Morty cried out and jumped to his feet, no longer concerned about the bullets panging off the office furnishings and walls.

He ran back to his old friend, who was sprawled over Ramsey's desk.

"Eddie! Eddie!"

In the darkness, Ramsey could hear Eddie moaning. No doubt he was dying. The sounds—and the smell of freshly spilled blood—reminded Ramsey of the war.

"You'll be all right, Eddie. You'll be all right," Morty kept saying over and over.

Ramsey raised his head again and got off a few more shots. But this time he didn't seem to hit anybody.

He glanced up at the big Ingram wall clock. Three and a half hours before the train would come in.

He wondered if he'd be alive then.

CHAPTER
★6★

1

Fifteen minutes before the gunfire started, banker Stufflebeam stood at the head of the town meeting hall, addressing all the other merchants of Congreve. All the merchants were drinking, and the hall smelled heavily of whiskey and hops.

"I know that we all cherish law and order as one of our true blessings in this country," Stufflebeam said, his pontifical words revealing the fact that he'd long considered himself a good candidate for governor. "And I'm all for it, too. But not at the cost of jeopardizing our relationship with the man who built this town."

"And the biggest investor in your bank!" laughed one of the men in the back.

Flushing, Stufflebeam said, "That has nothing to do with it!"

But now another man called out, "How much did he pay you to help him out?"

"I'm only doing my civic duty," Stufflebeam said carefully, trying to sound reasonable and in control of the situation. "I'm only thinking of our town. Do we really want to see it all shot up over young John Boyd? I don't think so."

Now the merchants fell silent.

"Do you want to go up against Robson's gunnies, Hank? Do you want to go up against George Boyd's drovers, Stewart?"

The men dropped their heads.

"I didn't think so," Stufflebeam went on. "Talk is one thing, but actually raising a rifle and risking your life—" He paused. "We're all family men here. And we're not gunslicks." He cleared his throat and leaned forward. "I say we march over to the jail in unison and demand that Ramsey let John Boyd go."

"How're we ever going to live with ourselves afterward?" said the haberdasher in the front row.

"We just have to look at it that we did the only thing we could to save the town," Stufflebeam said coolly.

Of course, he wasn't about to mention to any of these men the ten thousand dollar bonus George Boyd had promised him—if Stufflebeam could get John freed without a shot being fired.

"That's right," said Coleman, one of George Boyd's lawyers. "George doesn't want trouble. He only wants his son."

"Absolutely," Stoddard, the lawyer who'd inflicted the beating on John Boyd, agreed. "George doesn't want any trouble at all."

"You going to speak for us to Ramsey?" the grocer asked.

"I'll be glad to," Stufflebeam said, getting gubernatorial again, puffing up and looking out through the crowd.

The meeting hall was small. In the front was a stage. On

the left stood Old Glory and on the right the territorial flag. In the middle was a podium. Here Stufflebeam stood.

He was just about to say more when the rear door was thrown open and Rita Curry strode in.

Slung through her arm was a Winchester.

She walked straight up to the podium, raised the weapon and pointed it directly at Stufflebeam's head. "Sit down or I'll shoot you. It's my turn to speak."

A low muttering went through the crowd.

Had the woman lost her senses?

What the hell was going on here?

"You heard me," Rita said again, raising the Winchester now to aim it.

Stufflebeam, paling, did just as she ordered.

He fled the podium, hands fluttering nervously.

Rita got up on stage, walked to the podium and rested the Winchester against it.

When she looked out over the crowd, it was easy to see that she had been crying.

But despite that her voice sounded sure and confident. "Twenty minutes ago," she said to the group, "my father died."

Most of the men looked sad. Sam Curry had been a beloved figure in the community.

Only the lawyers Stoddard and Coleman seemed unmoved. They stared at their laps as if they didn't quite know how to behave.

"He died of a heart attack, as most of you have already guessed. A heart attack brought on—or I believe, anyway—with all the recent trouble over John Boyd."

For the first time, strong emotion was clear in her voice.

"But I don't want my father to have died in vain."

She looked out over the group again.

"Like most of you, until tonight I was all in favor of letting John Boyd walk free. One man's life isn't worth the destruction of this town."

She shook her head.

"Anyway, as I said, that's how I felt until tonight."

Stoddard said, "Don't go saying anything emotional, Rita. We're sorry about your father, but that's no reason to—"

"Until tonight," Rita went on as if Stoddard hadn't spoken at all, "I didn't understand why putting John Boyd on that train was so important to this town."

She could feel the first stirrings of the merchants.

Their pride in Congreve and themselves.

"If we don't put John Boyd on that train tonight, then we're not really a town at all. We're just a bunch of settlers who follow the law when it's convenient. If we're really civilized, if we believe all the things we say, then we'll put him on that train."

Coleman, the other lawyer, started to rise in his seat and object, but one of the merchants jumped up and pushed him back into his seat.

"Fortunately for my father, he was able to turn over the reins—at least temporarily—to an old friend of his, Matt Ramsey. Matt's determined to do the right thing, with or without our help. Right now he's got his deputy and Morty and Eddie—and that's all. And he's up against Robson and his gunnies and twenty of George Boyd's drovers."

Stufflebeam, looking more than ever like the too-prosperous banker he was, got to his feet and said, "Are you gentlemen going to let this woman stampede you into laying down your lives? Remember, you not only have businesses to protect—you've also got families and loved ones."

He tried to say more but he was shouted down by several merchants. He took his seat next to George Boyd's two lawyers, where he belonged.

Rita went on. "We've got five hours before the train. Can't we hold out for five hours? Can't all of us grab rifles and head for the sheriff's office?"

"You really think we can hold them off, Rita?" a man asked.

"Yes, I do."

"You really think we can get him on that train?" another called.

"If we stick with Matt Ramsey, we can."

By now you could feel the excitement in the men. They were obviously pleased with themselves now—proud. Up until a few minutes ago they'd had to look at themselves as cowards, men unwilling to face up to their responsibilities.

But now there was an almost festive atmosphere in the air.

They were no longer seated.

They were standing.

Getting themselves prepared mentally for what was certain to be a long and dangerous night.

Stufflebeam the banker and the two lawyers tried to talk the men down, get them to reconsider what they were doing, but obviously it was impossible at this point.

The men were going to act like men after all.

"This would make my father very proud," Rita Curry said. Tears had started rolling down her cheeks.

She hefted her Winchester and raised it above her head in a gesture of defiance.

She strode down the center aisle, pushing past Stufflebeam and the two lawyers.

The men, shouting and angry now, followed her out the front door.

2

Darkness.

Her first impression was that she was dead.

But if she was dead would she be able to hear her breath?

Would she see a faint line of light along the bottom of the door?

Closet.

She was in a closet.

And then she felt the raw burning pain in her throat.

He'd tried to strangle her.

The man from the other night. Thomas Peck.

The killer.

She'd come up here to blackmail him and—

Strangled her.

She tried to scream.

Nothing. No sound whatsoever.

Her voice gone utterly.

And even *trying* to scream caused so much pain in her throat she had to make tiny little fists to help endure it.

Darkness.

The dust made her sneeze.

He probably thought she was dead. Otherwise he would have bound her hands and feet.

She listened to the sounds of the hotel, faint beyond the door. Coughing. Laughter. Muffled conversation.

The door.

Of course.

She could reach up and let herself out.

If he didn't tie her up then he probably hadn't locked the door and—

She reached up and turned the knob.

Or tried to.

He had—the bastard—locked the door.

She considered trying to scream again, but the thought of all that pain dissuaded her.

She slumped in the corner.

She was no longer interested in money.

She just wanted to tell the law what Thomas Peck had done to Amanda Sayles the other night, and what he'd tried to do to her tonight.

Tell the law and watch the son of a bitch hang.

Right now, that would be a lot more satisfying than money.

Unfortunately, she couldn't figure out a way of getting out of this closet.

Desperate, she did something she hadn't done in years. Prayed.

Forgive me for being a whore, Father. But even whores get to ask you for favors sometimes, don't they? People think it's easy being a whore. All you do is lay on your back. But it's a lot tougher than that, Father, it really is. A lot of these guys, they don't even take baths and they've got warts and skin diseases and—

But, Father, listen, I'll consider going on the straight and narrow if you help me get out of this closet. I mean, I'm not making any guaranteed promises, you understand. But if you'll help me get out of here, I promise to at least consider being a good girl again.

So, all excited now that she'd communicated with God once again, and knowing that God was basically on her side, she reached up and tried the knob.

GUNDOWN

Locked.

Shit.

God, apparently, wasn't in any hurry to do her any big favors.

And that was when she heard the gunfire break out down the street from the hotel.

What the hell was going on, anyway?

3

Eddie was dead.

He lay over in a shadowy corner, blood flowing freely from his chest and face, the sour scents of death dancing around him like wraiths.

Morty kept crawling back over there to make sure the old black man was in fact dead.

But there could be no doubt.

No doubt at all, now.

Matt Ramsey and Deputy Quinn remained at the windows, firing at Robson and the other gunny.

Ramsey kept waiting for the sound of George Boyd's men to arrive as backups.

Deputy Quinn got off a shot and a good one. The gunny who'd been standing on the roof opposite the sheriff's office had made the mistake of leaning too far forward.

Deputy Quinn got him clean and confident.

The man tumbled from the roof with a certain degree of comic grace, like a circus performer intentionally adding a little trouble to a routine dive to make it look harder.

The man screamed all the way down.

"That leaves Robson," Deputy Quinn announced proudly.

Morty came back to the window where Ramsey squatted. "You can bet George Boyd's men are about five minutes away."

And just then, they heard the voices.

At first, they couldn't be sure who or what was making all that noise.

Then the light of torches began flickering against the dark buildings of the town.

And the rumble of human voices got louder, louder.

Down the street to the right, in the mouth of an alley, they saw the last of Robson's gunnies had struggled to his feet again and was trying to get a clear shot at the small, advancing army.

But the gunny was too late.

One of the rifle-bearing merchants shot the gunny two times in the chest before the man could even pull the trigger.

A huge roar went up from the crowd of merchants. It sounded as if they were in some kind of sporting contest and had just scored big.

They stood in the center of the street, just out in front of the jail, and they looked fearsome, fifteen men or so in the flapping yellow light of their torches, rifle stocks glistening in the glow.

They were like a spectral army, ready to spill blood on this night of a full moon.

Ramsey and the others went out to greet them, careful to keep watching for Robson, who had to be around somewhere.

"Evening, gentlemen," Ramsey smiled. "Out for a little target practice?"

The merchants laughed at that. Obviously, they relished their roles as gun-toters.

GUNDOWN

In the flickering torch light, Rita Curry stepped forward. She, too, carried a Winchester.

"You're not home with your father?"

She looked at him almost coldly. "He's dead, Matt."

The older Matt got, the more difficult it was to hear news of a close friend's death. Maybe that was because it meant that he, too, was getting closer to his own inevitable dying.

"I'm sorry, Rita."

"Nothing to be sorry for, Matt. You were a good friend to Dad. Look what you're doing here."

"You sure you want to be out here?"

Her gaze tightened. "I'm mad, Matt. Dad wouldn't be dead if George Boyd hadn't put all this pressure on him. Dad didn't want to see the whole town get shot up."

Ramsey smiled. "It's good to have you."

One of the merchants said, "We'd best be getting ready for them, Rita."

Ramsey nodded to the foothills on the east side of the town. "They'll be riding in any time now."

Rita said, "It's going to be pretty bloody, isn't it?"

"I'm afraid so," Ramsey said.

Rita nodded to the jail. "I've changed my mind. Maybe we could hang him and just get it over with. Then his father wouldn't have any reason to stay around here."

Ramsey felt shock at the suggestion. "But, Rita—he hasn't even been tried yet."

"He confessed, didn't he?"

And then abruptly, the men in the crowd began talking up the idea.

"Damn right, Sheriff!"

"And I'll go get the rope!"

"Time we showed George Boyd who's *really* boss around here!"

"He'd make a pretty sight, hanging from the big elm tree over by the livery stable!"

Ramsey had seen this happen many times. Give ordinary citizens some rifles and eventually they get transformed into killers. He'd seen this happen during the war, especially, when men too old to fight sometimes moved among the enemy dead, scavenging things off the corpses, on occasion even taking a scalp or two Indian-style. That was always the trouble with mobs. Ultimately they became more dangerous than the people they were pursuing.

And it didn't help that this group smelled as if it had been drinking for a long time.

"Let's take it easy," Ramsey said. "Let's take places along the street here and wait for Boyd to show up, all right?"

"Still say we should hang young John!" somebody shouted. "Be a pleasure to pay his old man back for all the things he's done to us over the years."

Ramsey glanced around at the merchants. "Sam Curry believed in law and order and so do I. Lynching isn't the way Sam did business. And it's not the way I do business either." This time he looked directly at Rita. "And I'd appreciate it if you'd all remember that."

With that, he waved the men to take up their shooting positions. George Boyd and his men would be here soon enough.

4

"Was she a virgin?"
"What the hell kind of question is that?"
"You don't want to answer it, do you?"

"Of course I don't want to answer it."

"Well, was she?"

Thomas Peck set down his drink and looked over at Sayles. The old man was drunk and asking him all sorts of intimate and morbid questions about Amanda.

"You didn't violate her, did you?"

Peck knew he'd have no rest until he gave the old man an answer. "No, I didn't."

Sayles glared at him. "That the truth?"

"That's the truth."

Sayles sighed, looking relieved. "I knew she was a good girl. She didn't give herself to John Boyd either."

That was something that Peck tried not to think about. Amanda giving her virginity to somebody else.

"She didn't," Sayles said, as if Peck had challenged him.

"I'm sure she didn't."

"And that's why he killed her. Right?"

"I suppose."

Sayles slammed his shot glass down on the table. They sat at a corner table. The saloon was nearly empty. Most people who'd ordinarily have been here were home, afraid to get caught up in the inevitable shoot-out between George Boyd and Matt Ramsey.

After several unrelieved hours of Sayles's mercurial company—he'd be high and happy and giggling part of the time, then down and dour and threatening the other part—Thomas Peck felt he needed to be alone.

Stretch his legs. Give his brain a relief from the constant emotional bombardment of Sayles.

Peck said, "I'm going to go for a walk."

"You mean I'm not invited?"

"I thought I'd walk up past the house where I grew up. It's something I'd rather do alone."

"You're sick of me, ain't ya?"

"Haven't you ever needed to be alone?"

"Fancy son of a bitch thinks he's too good for me."

Thomas Peck stood up. There was no reasoning with Sayles when he was like this. He couldn't imagine what Amanda had endured being raised by this man.

"I'll be back after a while."

"I ain't got no money."

"I left plenty of money with the barman. He'll give you whatever you want."

"A ham sandwich?"

"If you like."

"Rocky Mountain oysters?"

Thomas Peck sighed. It was like dealing with a small and hopelessly spoiled child. "As I said, anything you like. All you have to do is ask for it."

As Peck walked out through the batwing doors, the player piano started up in the background with "Camptown Races." Despite the happy tune, the music sounded curiously melancholy on the early evening air.

Peck stepped down into the dirt street. To his right, he could see the sheriff's office and glimpse the shadows of men crouched in the darkness, waiting for George Boyd and his men.

Thomas Peck headed in the opposite direction.

Memories accompanied him like ghosts. He saw the town of twenty years ago. He saw his handsome father in the expensive surrey and his beautiful mother in her finest clothes walking down the board sidewalks, the talk and envy of all the other women. They belonged back East, where they'd originally lived, but the scandal had forced them out here.

Even today, Thomas Peck wasn't sure what the scandal had been about. His father had been a lawyer and had fallen in love with a woman still in her teens. He had begun embezzling money to maintain the girl's lavish lifestyle. Once his embezzlement had been uncovered, the judge had given him the choice of leaving New York or going to prison. He packed up his family and came out here, to Congreve, where he started a successful law practice. Then, when Thomas was twelve, his father killed himself. Thomas still remembered the night. He'd been asleep, tossing sweatily in the nightmares his parents' arguments always inspired, and then abruptly some terrible echoing noise had awakened him. Gunshot. The sound seemed to fill every room in the vast house, echoing, echoing. Then his mother's screams and the colored maid's screams soon enough joining in. Then Thomas was up and running down the hall, panic like a giant wild bird in his chest. But Amie, the maid, wouldn't let him into his father's room. He'd never known before how strong the short, squat black woman really was. No matter what he did, he couldn't get past her. All he heard was his mother's terrible sobbing.

Three years later, his mother herself committed suicide. Officially, it was pronounced drowning, but his mother had been an excellent swimmer, and the river where she'd drowned had been shallow and still. He was fifteen years old. He had a decent education, money enough to start a business, and a certain civilized bearing one did not often find on the frontier.

And then he fell in love with Amanda Sayles.

Nothing like this had ever happened to him before. While he'd seen her around town most of his life, he suddenly became aware of her in a way that was almost painful, oppressive. Without her in his sight, he was miserable, wretched, and he began thinking of suicide just the way his father and mother had.

Fortunately, she returned his love. Oh, not with quite the same passion, the pure driven *need* that he felt, but she did like and love him, and she was amused and happy in his presence, and she did take his proposal of marriage quite seriously.

But then it changed.

He loved her *too* much, she said.

He gave her no room to be herself.

He wanted to be with her *always*.

She was afraid of this kind of love, she said.

She wasn't sure it was natural, she said.

He should have other interests. Hobbies. Passions. But no, there was just her and their time together and that wasn't—right.

He tried to be the man she wanted. He forced himself to have friends other than Amanda. He chose one or two nights a week to stay home and read so that she wouldn't feel he was constantly at her door. He no longer got angry when she went on a picnic with her church group of women.

But this pretense lasted only a short time.

Finally, he could take it no more. He told her he wanted to get married at once.

And it was then she told him that she no longer wanted to get married.

The days following that terrible night were murky in his mind now as he walked down the dusty street past the mansion where he'd been raised.

He went away, became a drummer, traveled, anything to escape her memory. He wrote her scores of letters and tore all of them up. Many times he'd started back toward

Congreve but stopped himself at the last moment.

By then he was afraid to see her. He knew how cruel and derisive she could be when she was angry, and he didn't think he could take that anymore.

Sometime during that period, she'd begun to see John Boyd. He could scarcely believe it. She'd always expressed such contempt for the Boyds and their ways. And John Boyd was hardly the "gentle" type of man she professed to care about so much.

He traveled even more widely. Now he went to Ohio and Kentucky, putting as much distance as possible between Amanda and himself.

There were days when he seemed to forget her entirely, didn't think of her at all. He seemed to be getting better, better.

But there always came a long and sleepless night when his old obsession returned.

It was on such a night that he abruptly decided to come back to Congreve.

He went to her home two nights ago, found her leaving with John Boyd on her arm. He followed them around all night.

John Boyd was drunk, barely able to walk. As they drew near the river, she lost patience with his drinking and they got into an argument.

She told John Boyd that she never wanted to see him again.

Hearing this, he felt his first hope in years. Amanda was throwing over John Boyd. She would welcome Peck back.

But after John Boyd fled, thinking that he'd killed Amanda, Peck went over to her. His intention was to revive her, but when he actually held her in his arms, he became furious, mad, and—

And he went insane.

That was the only way he could think of it now.

Insane.

He slapped her several times.

Pushed her to the ground.

He called her names that hurt her as much as fists.

And then he fell to the ground himself.

And began strangling her.

He felt her writhe beneath him.

Felt her fingers clawing at his face.

Saw in the moonlight how pain and fear had turned her beautiful face ugly.

This was not the Amanda he'd dreamt of so many nights.

This was some tawdry imitation.

And so he killed her.

In the moonlight, the mansion lay dark behind the iron gate. A huge padlock kept the curious away. He peered through the iron fence at the turrets and spires of the place. There was even a captain's walk.

Now, on the night, he thought he could hear, faint and ghostly, the sounds of his parents arguing.

How many nights he'd lain awake trying to blot out those sounds.

The grounds were overgrown. He could no longer see any of the "secret" paths where he'd played cowboys and Indians with himself and where he'd "hidden" from the colored maid when they'd played hide-and-go-seek.

He saw himself as a young boy.

Frail, pale, introspective.

People were always curious about what such little boys would be when they grew up.

And then another image came to mind.

Amanda.

Lying there in the grass by the river.

His hands on her throat.

This particular little boy had grown up to become a murderer.

Five minutes later, Thomas Peck hurried back to his hotel.

He had suddenly been overcome with worry about the whore he'd killed.

Had he in fact killed her?

He had the terrible sense that she was still alive.

She had broken her nails, clawing at the door. Three of her fingers were bloody stumps.

Every few minutes, she'd tried to scream but nothing had come out.

She'd even tried smashing against the door with her shoulder. But all that came of that was a badly bruised shoulder bone and a headache from where she'd accidentally struck the door with her skull.

Sometimes, she could hear people in the hallway.

Walking to the stairs. Talking and laughing.

How bright and fine and lucky these people seemed to her.

If only they knew that she was locked inside a small dark closet pleading for her very life.

Then they wouldn't care that she was a whore.

They'd come piling in as if she were their own daughter and help free her.

And then they'd find the terrible man Peck and teach him how to treat women, even those the community called whores.

Please, her mind would call out to the people in the hallway.

Please, as if they could read her mind and thoughts.

But they couldn't, of course, so she was left to the occasional attempt to bash in the door or call out.

Now she heard more footsteps in the hall.

Coming briskly toward the room.

The steps of a man; definitely a man.

Oh, Sada, she thought. *Sada, this is the one who will rescue you. I know it. Oh, please make it the one, Lord. Please make it the one.*

A key in the door to this room.

Turning, turning.

The door opening, the hinges creaking for need of oil.

Footsteps heavier now, coming closer, closer.

A hand on the knob of the closet door, and the door opening, and—

She sat there staring up at him.

She looked like a frightened, scruffy little girl.

And she was, of course, very much alive.

He took his .45 from his holster and pointed it directly at her.

He waved for her to stand up and to come out into the room.

She was two steps in the room when he slapped her very hard across the face. Hard enough to slam her back against the frame of the closet door.

She made a whimpering voice and tried to say something, but nothing came out, and it was then he realized that his strangling her had left her mute.

He grabbed her and hurled her across the room where she fell backward onto the bed.

The room was in deep shadow. The only light came from streetlamps. The windows were closed. The room was like a tomb.

The idea of her muteness amused him. "Go ahead and scream, why don't you?" he said.

She only shook her head miserably.

"You were going to turn me over for a few dollars. Why don't you scream out for the sheriff now?"

He drew ever closer to her.

And it was then that he slid his gun back into his holster and took from somewhere inside his suit coat a long and shining bowie knife.

"Beautiful, isn't it? I had it made for me in Chicago. The man who did it is a real craftsman. Takes great pride in his work."

He smiled, touching his thumb to the sharp edge of the knife. "And I take great pride in my work, too. That's why—this time—I'm going to make certain that I do it right." He shook his head. "No mistakes this time. I promise you."

"Please."

The word came out of her pathetically.

It almost wasn't a word at all.

Just this wispy, plaintive little sound.

"Please."

He smiled again.

"If you'd only been nice to me," he said. "People don't know how little I want. Just to be—nice. To be my friend. That's all I've ever asked from anybody. But—"

He started toward the bed then.

The knife ready.

He wanted the job done with.

He wanted away from Congreve now.

"Please."

Again the pathetic rasp.

He was at the bed.

Savagely, his hand shot out and grabbed her hair, holding her steady.

He put the knife to her throat.

And was about to make a long, slashing motion when—

—a knock came on the door.

He froze.

He saw hope shine ridiculous in her eyes. He resented seeing the hope there.

The knock again.

This time, a voice. "Thomas. You in there?"

It was Robert Sayles.

What the hell was he doing here?

Peck straightened up. He made a threatening face at Sada and then stepped back from the bed.

And then, enraged, he went to answer the door.

He opened it only a crack. "Yes, Robert?"

"Wondered where the hell you went to?"

"I told you I'd be back."

"I got—lonely. You know. Ain't got my daughter or anything anymore."

Sayles was drunk and in his weepy mood again.

"You go back to the saloon and wait for me."

"How come you won't invite me in?"

"You just go back there and wait, all right?"

"George Boyd's men're coming. That's the word now. Going to be a big shoot-out."

He glanced back over his shoulder.

Sada was still on the bed, though he could tell by the way her eyes moved around that she was looking for some chance of escape.

"How long you gonna be?"

"Not long."

"You promise?"

God. The man was a five-year-old. "I promise."

"Still don't see why I can't come in."

Peck could no longer talk to the man without completely losing his temper. He closed the door on Sayles.

When he turned back to the bed, he saw that she was gone.

Hiding somewhere in the room.

He thought of the hide-and-go-seek games he used to play with his colored nanny.

They'd been fun then; why not now?

He started searching for Sada.

5

Within ten minutes, the small army of merchants had found rifle positions for themselves. Some chose rooftops; some chose alleyways and doorways; others chose windows in their own shops. Put together, this was a formidable array of firepower.

Inside the sheriff's office, Ramsey went back to the jail cell where John Boyd sat.

Still smarting from his beating, Boyd sat up slowly, grimacing as he did so.

Ramsey held a lantern up for light.

"Your father's coming," Ramsey said.

Boyd smiled. "I knew he would."

"You could stop him."

"Why would I want to do that?"

"Because of what's going to happen to this town."

"I can't get a fair trial."

"I think you know you can; I think you just want an excuse."

Boyd sat on the edge of his cot, rubbing his face. He looked up at Ramsey. "This is all like a nightmare."

"I imagine it is."

"I don't even remember killing her."

"You were pretty drunk, I'm told."

Boyd sighed.

"Why don't you stop your father, son? There's no need for all this killing."

Boyd hung his head, ran comblike fingers through his hair. "I couldn't stop him now. It's a point of pride with him. He wants his son back." Boyd glanced up and smiled. "Even if I didn't want to go, he'd take me."

Ramsey grimaced. "Well, then, you'd better get ready for some excitement. Your father and his men are going to be along any time now."

With that, Ramsey took the lantern and went back up front.

"Listen," Deputy Quinn said five minutes later.

There were four of them in the sheriff's office, each at a different window—Ramsey, Quinn, Morty and Rita. Each had a carbine. Each was ready.

After her outburst at the meeting hall about hanging John Boyd now, Ramsey saw that Rita was suffering under the strain of her father's death. He'd taken her aside and gently reminded her that her father had been a law-and-order man and would not have approved of lynching under any circumstances. Tearfully, Rita had agreed with him.

"You hear something?" Morty asked.

"Listen," Quinn said again.

GUNDOWN 121

And then they all heard it—the steady footfall of iron shoes against hard-packed earth.

In the nighttime stillness, the sound of the horse's hooves was loud and distinct.

"One man," Ramsey said.

"And I'll bet I know who it is," Rita said.

"Robson," Morty said.

And it was then that Harry Robson appeared. He rode a lone roan. In the lantern glow of the street, he was a burly, shadowy figure. He carried a Winchester laid across his saddle horn.

When he got to the sheriff's office, he stopped.

"I know you're in there, Ramsey," Robson said. "Come out so we can talk."

"Don't go out there, Matt," Morty said. "Could be a trap of some kind."

"George Boyd wants me to make you an offer," Robson said.

Dramatically, he raised his Winchester then dropped it to the dusty earth.

"All I want is to talk," he said.

Ramsey stood up. His knees ached from crouching. He was almost grateful for standing.

"I'll be right back," he said to the other three.

"I wouldn't do it, Matt," Deputy Quinn said. "That Robson is one bad fellow."

Ramsey nodded and went out into the night, his boots loud on the boards of the sidewalk.

"You wanted to see me?" Ramsey said, still standing in the shadows of the overhang.

"That's right, Sheriff. I wanted to see you." As usual, Robson managed to sound sarcastic as he spoke.

He climbed down from his horse, a surprisingly graceful

man given his bulk, then walked out to the center of the street and stood there.

He pulled the flap of his suit jacket back. A pearl-handled .45 rode a black holster.

"Boyd's idea was for me and you to finish this ourselves," Robson said. "If I win, we take the kid. If you win—" He smiled. "Well, seeing as how I won't be around, I guess I won't much care what happens if you win."

Ramsey felt his heart begin to pound. His palms and the bottoms of his feet got wet with icy sweat.

Robson was a professional gunny. Everything was in his favor.

"How about it, Ramsey?" Robson said.

"Don't do it, Matt!" Rita Curry yelled out. "Let me shoot him right now."

In the moonlight, Ramsey could see the barrel of her carbine glinting.

"I'll take care of this, Rita. Just calm down."

"You ever going to move off the walk, lawman?" Robson said.

Ramsey took his first two steps onto the dusty ground. His right hand started moving toward the gun strapped around his waist.

"You scared, Ramsey?"

Ramsey said nothing, just kept edging into the street.

"I'm told that when men face me, they get all fluttery. Start to sweat a lot and can't catch their breath. Their eyes even go out of focus a little."

He was good at this, Robson was, talking a man into fear even when he felt plenty of fear already.

The two men fanned out, facing each other.

"Any time you're ready," Robson said.

Ramsey knew he had only one chance against a gunny

GUNDOWN

like Robson. But even as he quickly formulated his plan, he also knew that he had little chance of pulling it off.

"Kill him, Sheriff!"

"You don't take any of his crap, Sheriff!"

"I'll shoot him right now if you want me to!"

These were the voices of the hidden merchants who were watching the gunfight.

On the night, their voices were angry and slurred with alcohol. Ramsey had to wonder just how useful they'd be when they were liquored up this way.

"I'll handle this," Ramsey said. "You just sit still."

There were a few more muttered curses and oaths, but finally the merchants fell silent again.

Ramsey and Robson were now in the center of the street. No longer moving. Just watching each other in the flickering lamplight.

"Even had a man drop a gun on me once," Robson said, laughing. "That was some sight. He went to pull his gun, but he was so scared he dropped it right on the ground." Robson's chuckle sounded genuine.

Ramsey steeled himself as much as possible. He knew what Robson was doing. Distracting him with these words. He'd lull Ramsey into listening and then suddenly Robson's gun would flash in his hand and—

"Any time you're ready," Ramsey said.

His voice sounded much surer and more self-confident than he felt. He'd made it through a long and bloody war and innumerable battles following the war—but facing a professional gunny was something else entirely.

"I imagine your friends in all those windows are real proud of you," Robson said. "Standing up to a man like me. Real proud. Hell, if you beat me, Sheriff, they'll probably ask you to stay on permanently, and they'll probably even give you a raise." He laughed. "Now wouldn't that be nice?" Get to spend the rest of your life in a burg like Congreve? My oh my, Sheriff, aren't we the lucky one?"

And then Ramsey saw it, the lightning flash of Robson's pistol leaving his holster.

Then Robson was raising his weapon—starting to fire it—flame erupting yellow-orange from the barrel and—

Ramsey, just as he'd planned, dove headfirst for the dirt, as if he were jumping into deep water.

Pain slammed through his jaw as his chin slammed the dirt.

He heard Robson's shots erupt like cannon fire in the night.

And then Ramsey let loose with his own gunfire, his .45 slamming three quick bullets into Robson's chest.

Robson still couldn't find Ramsey. As the lead ripped through his heart and lungs, Robson was still swiveling his head for sight of the lawman.

Just as Ramsey had hoped, his hitting the dirt had confused Robson. In the shadowy night, Robson's eyes hadn't been able to adjust to the lawman dropping to the ground. Robson had fired high and uselessly, while Ramsey's bullets had found their home right off.

Robson pitched over backward.

When he struck the earth, Ramsey, now scrambling to his feet, could see the dark blood spreading over the bulky man's chest.

There was no doubt about it.

Robson was dead.

The windows erupted with half-drunken calls of appreciation for what Ramsey had been able to do.

Rita came running out, over to Ramsey. She slid her arm around him and hugged him like a little girl fondly embracing a long-absent father. "I'm so glad you're all right, Matt."

From an alley at the opposite end of the street, Ramsey heard sharp hoofbeats as a horse was ridden fast out of town.

This would be George Boyd's spy.

Within minutes, Boyd would be told what had happened here.

Then he and his men would come to town ready for a last-ditch fight.

There were three hours to go before the train arrived.

They just might be the longest three hours in Matt Ramsey's lifetime.

6

This had turned into more of a game than Thomas Peck had wanted.

After five minutes, he had still not found Sada. The only thing he was certain of was that she was still in the room—somewhere.

But where?

He'd looked under the bed, in the closet, behind the bureau. She was in none of these places. Nor was she behind the curtains.

She was somewhere in the room but—where?

And then he heard it.

Just outside the window.

Heart pounding, he raced to the curtains, threw them back.

He hadn't thought of the window. It was open three inches. That's where she'd gone. The fire escape.

He threw open the window and stuck his head out.

There she was, all right, crouched several feet above him on the catwalk of the fire escape.

Cowering.

Apparently too frightened to move.

He crawled outside, weapon drawn.

"You come down here," he said. "And right now."

He might have been talking to a naughty child. He couldn't afford to speak above a whisper.

Only moonlight gave the alley illumination. He could smell sweet-sour garbage somewhere in the darkness, and the unmistakable scent of horseshit from the livery stable.

"Come on, now."

"You're going to hurt me." Her voice was raspy, barely a whisper, from the strangling.

"I'm not going to hurt you."

"Yes, you are. You said you were."

Both of them spoke in whispers.

He was afraid that one of the hotel residents would get nosy and stick his head out the window. He would see that Thomas Peck held a gun on the cowering girl. And he would immediately run and get the sheriff.

"Come on, now."

"If you promise not to hurt me, I'll forget about what I saw."

"Let's talk inside."

Stay calm. Sound peaceful. Don't scare her.

He slipped the gun back into his holster.

Extended his hand out to her. "There's no reason we can't be friends."

"Really?"

"Really."

She stared at his hand as if she weren't quite sure what it was.

GUNDOWN 127

"I'm scared."

"No reason to be."

He said nothing. Just watched her.

She stood up. He could see that she was stiff from crouching.

But she didn't take the first step down. She just stood there, watching him.

He put his hand out again.

"Please," he said.

She took her first step.

It was like watching some cripple learn to walk again.

"Easy, now," he said, as if he were her very best friend and didn't want to see her get hurt.

She took her second step.

He could see how scared she was. Apparently, nobody had ever tried to kill her before. In a curious way, he found that surprising. Given her naturally predatory instincts, he thought she'd have gotten herself into deep trouble many times.

And then he grabbed her.

She hadn't been expecting it, obviously. He grabbed her wrist, and before she had time to scream, he had covered her mouth with his wide hand.

She tried to scream behind his hand, but the sound was almost completely muffled.

She tried to bite his hand but that didn't work either. It only made him clamp down all the harder.

Dragging her inside was not easy, and several times he slammed her head against the window frame.

Once he got soundly on the floor again and had yanked the drapes closed, he lifted his gun and put the barrel right next to her head.

"You son of a bitch," she said when he took his gun away.

"You must really want to die."

"You son of a bitch," she said again.

But he noticed that she was still whispering.

Obviously, she knew he'd kill her if she tried to scream or anything like that. Plus, he thought, she was still suffering from the strangling. He smiled.

"I want you to go over on the bed and lay down," he said.

"For what?"

"You'll find out."

For the first time tonight, he became aware of her as a woman. He saw how her breasts pushed against the cotton of her dress, how her soft buttocks felt against his thighs.

He pushed her toward the bed.

She fell facedown, whimpering again.

He lay on top of her.

She began to writhe, and he felt himself start to stir sexually.

"What do you want?"

And for a moment, he wasn't sure what he wanted—pleasure or business.

He brought the gun down hard across the back of her skull.

He felt her go flaccid beneath him.

Blood began to leak from a small red hole he could see beneath her hair.

He stood up.

He turned her over so that she faced him. Despite himself, he found his eyes falling once again to her breasts.

Maybe there would be time for—

But he shook his head and set to work.

This time when he strangled her, he made certain that there was no breath left in her chest.

When he was finished, he lifted her off the bed, her head still leaking blood, and carried her quickly over to the closet before blood could stain the carpet. He cupped his free hand under her skull.

Finished, the door closed, he went over and stood by the window.

He could hear the first, faint thundering of George Boyd's men as they came riding into town.

And then there was gunfire.

They were too far away to hit anybody, Boyd's men were, but they just wanted the townspeople to know that there were a lot of them and that they were here to free young John Boyd.

The closer they drew to town, the more gunfire he heard on the soft night air.

He picked up his hat, went to the hotel door, opened it, and stepped out into the hallway.

He looked around and saw nobody.

Feeling good now—this time the bitch Sada was dead for sure—he started off down the hall.

After he heard Thomas Peck's footsteps retreating down the front stairs, Robert Sayles stepped out from the door leading to the back stairs.

He had been standing there for twenty minutes.

Something about the way Thomas Peck had tried to get rid of him earlier had made Sayles curious.

What had been going on in Peck's room, anyway?

Sayles looked both ways in the hall. Then he went over to Peck's door and tried the lock.

Damn.

He'd need a key.

Then Sayles remembered the fire escape. It ought to be easy enough to climb in Peck's window.

Then he could find out for sure why Peck had been acting so mysterious when Sayles had knocked on the door a little while ago.

Sayles sensed that something was terribly, terribly wrong.

CHAPTER ★7★

1

George Boyd's men came riding straight down Main, the muzzle fire from their handguns sparking the night air like fireworks. Some of their horses bucked and protested at the loud noises the weapons made, but for the most part Boyd's men shot their way into town without any trouble.

Obviously, they hadn't counted on Ramsey getting up any significant force of townspeople. Boyd's men were clearly surprised when gunfire from at least a dozen directions greeted them.

From windows, from doorways, from rooftops, from buggies came carbine fire that started killing Boyd's men immediately.

There was no time for Boyd or his men to make any readjustment. They were trapped in a crossfire and all they could do was shoot back and hope for the best.

In the faint moonlight—the lamps having already been shot out—dead riders started pitching from their horses.

As Ramsey crouched next to the jail window, taking shot after shot, the carnage in the street started to remind him of a battle in the recent war, where animals and men alike died in pools of their own blood.

Either way Boyd's men tried to go, gunfire greeted them.

The merchants grew bolder.

They appeared out of the shadows, their carbines glinting in the moonlight.

Boyd's men were drovers, not gunnies, so they were afraid now that they'd reached town.

Now some of the merchants started walking into the street toward the huge, reeking pile of human and animal bodies that was already attracting flies and the black carrion birds of the West.

The merchants showed the drovers no compassion.

Even a drover who threw down his gun and put his hands up in the air was shot three times in the chest by the local tailor. Years of resentment had built up, and this resentment was all being expressed here tonight.

Ramsey came running out from the sheriff's office, stopping the merchants before they killed any more drovers.

"That's enough!" Ramsey shouted to a small cluster of merchants who were holding two drovers in the center of the street.

"We got a right to kill 'em, Ramsey," one merchant said drunkenly. "They rode into town with their guns out."

Ramsey stepped up to the merchants and leveled his own rifle at them. He nodded to the street.

There were at least fifteen dead bodies.

And that wasn't counting the horses.

"Seems like we've had enough killing for the night," Ramsey said.

"Boyd's been askin' for this for years," someone said.

"Maybe he has," Ramsey said. "But right now there's been enough bloodshed for one night."

"Where is Boyd, anyway?" someone asked.

From the sheriff's office, Rita Curry came, and then Morty and Deputy Quinn.

As they approached, Quinn asked the same question. "I haven't seen Boyd anywhere, have you?"

Ramsey shook his head.

Then somebody shouted. "Over here! Behind the watering trough!"

A torch was hoisted, its flame flapping on the breeze. The man carrying it led a small procession down the dusty street to the trough.

Behind it, Ramsey found George Boyd.

Two bullets—one apparently in the stomach—had left the once-virile man ashen and scarcely able to move. His eyes glowed with the sickness of impending death. The hand that reached out for Ramsey looked almost arthritic.

"Finish him," someone said.

And behind Ramsey the butcher took his Navy Colt and aimed it directly at George Boyd's face.

Ramsey slapped the gun from the man's hand.

He looked around at the faces of the men. It was an ugly sight, really, for otherwise reasonable men had been turned into killers by alcohol and rage. He'd seen this many times in the war, how men could get pumped up with hatred to the point that they ceased to be men at all. They were animals of the lowest order.

Ramsey nodded to Deputy Quinn. "Why don't you get these men out of here?"

"This is our town, too," someone said angrily.

Ramsey nodded to Quinn again.

After many sarcastic comments, the men followed Quinn

down the street. They were like youngsters who were only reluctantly following an older brother.

Now only Rita Curry and Ramsey remained standing over George Boyd.

She looked down at him and shook her head. "I wish I felt more like helping you, George."

Boyd's dried, caked mouth opened to say something but no words came out.

"My father might still be alive if it wasn't for you," she said.

Ramsey thought of stopping her but decided that he owed her at least this.

She should be able to say what she felt.

"You kept this town under your thumb too long," she said. "The people who used to love you and respect you hate you now. And that isn't a good thing to take to your grave."

In the moonlight, she looked older than her years, hard now and used up.

She took a few steps closer to Boyd, stopped and then shook her head again.

"Maybe it's a good thing your boy's going to hang, because otherwise he would have kept this town in fear just the way you did."

Once more, George Boyd raised a trembling, ghostly hand and tried to speak. But the words wouldn't come this time either.

And then she broke, started sobbing. "You killed my father!" she cried. "You killed my father!"

Ramsey led her away to the center of the street.

She kept glancing back over her shoulder at Boyd.

Morty came over from the front of the sheriff's office and took her by the arm and guided her gently back to the porch.

GUNDOWN 135

Ramsey went back to George Boyd.

The doctor, who had first been treating two merchants who'd been slightly injured, was now kneeling next to George Boyd.

When Ramsey got there, the doctor looked up and said, "Couple of minutes and he'll be gone."

The doctor stood up, hefting his small black leather bag as he did so. "Better go see if there's anybody I can do something for."

With that, he doffed his homburg.

"How about getting him to a bed?" Ramsey said.

"Won't be time."

"Anything you can do for his pain?"

The look on George Boyd's face revealed the incredible gut-shot pain he must be feeling.

The doctor's voice softened. " 'Fraid not, Ramsey. Much as I detest the son of a bitch, I'd give him something for the pain if I had something. But I'm afraid I don't."

And with that, the doctor doffed his hat again and left.

Ramsey stood over Boyd.

Boyd stared up at him, tried to speak.

Ramsey couldn't understand the words.

Boyd once more raised his hand and beckoned Ramsey closer.

Ramsey knelt down next to the man.

"My son," Boyd rasped.

"Yes."

"He didn't kill Amanda."

Ramsey sighed. "He'll get a fair trial."

"He didn't kill her."

Ramsey just shrugged. "You should just rest."

The burning eyes of death shone even more fiercely now.

"I know my son, Ramsey. I know all the things he's done—but I'm sure he didn't kill her. I'm sure of it."

He reached out and grasped Ramsey's elbow.

The grasp was surprisingly strong.

"I don't want to die thinking he's going to hang for something he didn't do."

Ramsey looked down at the man, feeling sorrier for him than he wanted to.

"I'll make sure he gets a fair trial," Ramsey said.

A fairer trial than Amanda Sayles got; she didn't get any trial at all, Ramsey thought.

"Ramsey?"

"Yes."

"Finish me, will you?"

"I can't do that."

"You don't know what the pain's like."

And just then, Boyd made an animal wailing noise that raised the hairs on the back of Ramsey's neck.

"Ramsey."

"What?"

"Please—finish me."

Ramsey was about to again say he couldn't do anything like that when George Boyd gave one last wrenching gasp. His head fell to the left so abruptly it seemed that his neck had been broken.

No doubt about what had just happened.

George Boyd had died.

Ramsey was just about to lean forward and close the man's staring eyes when he heard the gunfire erupt from the front of the jail.

Then there were shouts and the sound of feet running and more gunfire.

He saw Deputy Quinn come stumbling out from the

office, clutching a spreading red smear on the arm of his blue work shirt.

Somebody had shot him.

Quinn pitched forward to the dusty street.

Now there was no time to worry about closing Boyd's eyes.

Ramsey drew his gun and started running toward the sheriff's office.

2

A couple of times Sayles felt as if somebody was watching him. He stopped and looked around before climbing in through the fire-escape window leading to Thomas Peck's room.

But then, seeing nobody peeking through curtains, he shrugged and went inside.

The room was dark.

Once inside, he stumbled against a chair.

The noise was unnaturally loud now that all the gunfire had died down at the other end of town.

He wondered if anybody in any of the adjoining rooms had heard him.

Behind him, the sheer white curtains billowed out in ghostly fashion; ahead of him, deep shadows crouched in every corner, as if waiting to spring on him.

He felt himself trembling.

He'd never pretended to be a brave man.

He heard a sound in the hallway and froze.

Flattened himself against the wall.

Heart hammering.

Shoe leather squeaked in the hallway outside. A man

whistled on his way to the other end of the hall.

Had Thomas Peck come back? How would he ever explain to Peck what he was doing in this room?

The shoe leather—and the man—passed by. Several doors down, a key clicked in a lock.

Sayles's breath was now less ragged. His heart beat more slowly. He could move again without feeling as if his knees would buckle beneath him.

He started looking around, and it was then he stepped in something sticky on the rug.

He bent down and touched a finger to the sticky area and then brought his finger back up to his eyes for inspection.

Little doubt of what it was. Blood.

So Thomas Peck had been up to something. But what?

He stood up, knees cracking, and searched through the gloom for more signs of blood.

For the next five minutes, he looked around the room but found no more blood.

He checked out the bureau drawers and then checked out the shelves next to the closet. Nothing.

In front of the closet, he found more blood. It led straight to the closet door.

Once again, he felt nervous. What was he going to find behind the closet door?

He put his hand forward to the knob.

He was about to find out.

He turned the knob and edged the door open and looked inside.

Thomas Peck was halfway to the sheriff's office when he realized he'd dropped his good leather wallet. Without it, he had no money whatsoever.

And he knew just exactly where he'd left it.

He turned in the street now, heading back to the hotel. Without quite knowing why, a sense of dread came over him, a deep and sickening anxiety.

He sensed that something was suddenly, profoundly wrong.

He wished he knew what it was.

The stench was the worst part.

Robert Sayles wished he'd lit a lantern before opening the closet door.

Here he was staring into gloom so deep and so black it was like staring down a well—and he didn't know what he was looking at.

He could only guess.

He tried not to think about it.

Leaving the closet door ajar, he went back to the bureau and got the lantern.

Once he got it lit, its warm glow spreading softly across the walls of the room, he went straight back to the closet.

Now he didn't have to wonder about what he was smelling anymore.

He'd always heard they smelled bad following a violent death.

He supposed even his own little Amanda had smelled bad.

He leaned in with the lantern and took his first good look at her face.

She'd been hit hard on the head, and blood was still oozing from the wound.

She'd also been strangled, neck snapped, her tongue lolled out the right side of her mouth, and her eyes were open, staring accusingly up at him.

As if he could have prevented it in some way.

He tried not to look at her nice naked breasts. It wasn't

proper. It was downright disrespectful. Even if she had been a whore.

And then he realized something.

If she'd been strangled—and Amanda had been strangled—then that meant that the man who'd done it was . . .

Sayles didn't have time to turn completely around when the door opened behind him.

He'd been so engrossed in staring at the dead girl that he hadn't heard the other man in the hall. Nor heard him opening the door.

Nor heard him closing the door and taking out his .45.

"Just ease on out of there, Robert," Thomas Peck said.

Sayles took one last look at the dead girl then started to move away from the closet.

"You recognize her, Robert?"

Sayles grunted something.

"A whore named Sada."

Sayles now turned around and faced him.

"I—I was feeling lonely so I had her come up here."

Thomas Peck was studying Sayles's face, obviously trying to get some sense of the man's thoughts.

"I know I shouldn't have done something like that," Peck said. "But I've been so lonely lately—" He shook his head.

"You killed her," Sayles said.

"I was coming to that part."

"And put her in the closet."

"She tried to rob me. I'd dozed off to sleep, and when I woke up, I found her going through my wallet."

"But you killed her."

"It was an accident."

Then Sayles said, and with a great sense of significance, "You strangled her."

"I'm aware of that."

GUNDOWN

"Amanda was strangled."

"I know that."

"John Boyd didn't strangle her. You did."

Thomas Peck said nothing. Simply looked at the other man. He sighed then. It was a weary sigh, an old man's sigh. "I was afraid you were going to come to that conclusion."

"You strangled my little Amanda."

Thomas Peck said, "I loved her, Robert. You know that."

"You killed her." By now Sayles sounded hopelessly insane.

"I went to the river the other night to tell her that I still loved her and still wanted to marry her and she treated me as if—" Thomas Peck shook his head miserably. "She treated me as if I were some kind of madman or something."

Sayles started walking toward him.

"Don't be foolish, Robert. I've got a gun on you."

"You killed my daughter."

"I loved your daughter, Robert. The problem was, she didn't understand that."

"You didn't love her. You killed her."

"Only because—" Thomas Peck looked at the other man with a mixture of pity and contempt. "I wouldn't expect you to understand, Robert."

"I'm going to tell Ramsey."

Peck raised the .45. "I'm afraid you aren't, Robert. I'm afraid you're going in the closet with the whore."

Sayles lunged for him.

Thomas Peck's first instinct was to shoot, but he knew that he couldn't. Gunfire would bring people running. People who'd have a lot of questions to ask.

Sayles rammed into him hard enough to knock them both to the floor. For the next few minutes, they wrestled around,

Sayles getting in a punch or two then Peck getting in a punch or two.

Sayles had no hesitation about fighting dirty, his teeth taking a deep gouge out of Peck's neck, his right knee several times finding Peck's groin.

Thomas Peck was surprised. He'd expected the old man to be frail. But Sayles fought with a ferocity born of true rage—Thomas Peck was, after all, the man who'd murdered his daughter.

The fight went on a minute longer, the men rolling back and forth, trading punches in the wide empty space between bureau and bed.

And then finally Thomas Peck got in a position to use the walnut handle of his .45, which he brought down with quick, keen anger on the back of Robert Sayles's skull.

The old man pitched face forward, drained of all stamina and purpose now, making a small whimpering animal noise of pain as he slid into unconsciousness.

Thomas Peck stood up a moment, catching his breath. A chill sweat covered him now, his heart pounding from the anxiety that was coming around again.

He leaned over and got the old man by the ankles and started dragging him toward the closet.

He was halfway there when he froze. Footsteps were coming down the hall toward his room.

He took out his revolver and pointed it at the door.

Who was coming down the hall so quickly? And for what reason?

He heard the runner pause and begin knocking thunderously on the door of the room next to Peck's.

A male voice shouted, "If you want to see a lynching, get to the sheriff's office fast! They just dragged out the Boyd kid and are going to hang him over by the park!"

The man's exultation was no pretense. His voice carried pure high excitement, the kind you hear in a youngster's voice when the circus rolls into town.

To him, a lynching was obviously a good and wondrous event, and he wanted to share his glee with others—hence his knocking on the door.

He next came to Peck's door and pounded on it with similar exuberance. "If you want to see a lynching, better hurry on over to the sheriff's office while the kid's still alive! You won't have long!"

Peck stood listening in the middle of his room. For the first time this evening, he relaxed. He even allowed himself a small smile.

Things had finally broken his way.

The man he hated so much, the man who'd stolen his woman—he wouldn't even have to touch him now.

A crazed mob was going to do that for him.

A man like Thomas Peck couldn't get much luckier than that.

He finished dragging Robert Sayles into the closet, pushing aside the whore and packing Sayles in right next to her.

After closing the door, his first thought was of a nice cold beer.

He probably shouldn't stop for one before going to the jail, but given everything that had happened tonight, he felt badly in need of one.

He hurried to the saloon.

3

"Where is it?"

"I'm not going to tell you."

"You tell us where it is or we'll put a bullet clean through your head."

Ramsey said nothing.

After hearing gunshots earlier, he'd rushed inside the office to see what was going on.

Several merchants—still enjoying the exhilaration of killing George Boyd's men—had struggled with Deputy Quinn, shooting him in the arm and trying to get the jail key from him so they could take John Boyd out of his cell and down the street to the big oak tree where they planned to hang him.

Deputy Quinn hadn't given them the key nor told them where they could find it.

Now the merchants had both Ramsey and Quinn tied to chairs in the front office, and they were demanding that Ramsey tell them where the key was. Mort Boyd was also tied up.

Quinn was wincing from the gunshot in his arm.

"You tellin' me you don't think he should be hanged?" a drunken merchant spat in Ramsey's face.

"What I'm telling you is that we've got to abide by the law," Ramsey said.

"He killed her."

"Maybe he did," Ramsey said. "But he still deserves a trial."

"She didn't get any trial."

"No," Ramsey said, trying to sound calm and reasonable, "no, she didn't."

"Then why should he?"

"Because my father worked hard all his life at keeping this a law-abiding town."

Rita Curry's soft voice was a contrast to the harsh, boozy voices of the men.

She'd just stepped through the front door of the sheriff's office. She toted a Winchester, aimed directly at the merchant who was bent over Ramsey, and she looked as if she had every intention of using it if necessary.

"Get away from him, Lem," she said.

"Now, Rita. You just get on home and—"

"You heard what I said, Lem."

"But, Rita, all we want is—"

"I know what you want. It's what I wanted, too, but then Matt convinced me that this isn't what my father would have wanted at all."

"But, Rita—"

The other merchants in the office now started to fan out as she came deeper into the room.

None of them seemed to have any doubt that she'd actually shoot.

"They'll let him off at a trial," one of the other merchants said. He was trying to sound sensible, to reason with her. "Boyd's lawyers will make out that it was all somehow a terrible accident, and then Boyd'll be free to go wherever he wants. You know how it is with the Boyds, Rita."

She waved the man away from Ramsey. "Boyd's father is dead. John Boyd doesn't have any power anymore."

"Yeah, but he'll have the family money to bribe the jury if necessary," another man said.

"And after you lynch him, what happens?" Rita said. "Are you going to start lynching every prisoner you don't like?"

"This is a special case, Rita," one of the men said.

"Untie him," Rita said, nodding to Ramsey.

"Now, Rita—" one of the merchants said.

"You heard me. Untie him."

Ramsey saw the man behind her and started to shout, but it was already too late.

The man pushed Rita through the door, knocking her into the desk.

The Winchester misfired with a terrible thundering echo, knocking down a huge piece of plaster to the right of the gun rack.

Rita spun around, trying to right herself, but it did no good.

The man coming through the door grabbed her by the shoulders and hurled her into the wall.

The Winchester fell from her hands to the floor.

The man took Rita in his hands as if she were a small, disobedient child, marched her across the room and sat her down on an empty chair.

"Tie her up," he said.

Now the man who'd been talking to Ramsey started again. "Wouldn't you like to just ride out of Congreve, Sheriff?"

Ramsey nodded. "Right now, that sounds pretty good to me."

"Just get on your horse and keep riding? And not worry about anything that's going on here? Doesn't that sound nice?"

"Very nice."

"Then will you do it if we untie you?"

"I tell you where the key is?"

"Right."

"And then I get on my horse and ride out."

"With a fifty-dollar gold piece in your pocket to sweeten the deal."

Ramsey looked at Rita. "Right now, that sounds pretty good."

"Then you'll do it?"

"Afraid I can't."

"Why not?"

"It's like Rita said. We owe it to her father to keep law and order in this town."

The man slapped him.

Ramsey knew that the night had now taken an even worse turn. Not only was the drunken crowd going to hang a prisoner, they were going to rough up—maybe even kill—a lawman who stood in their way.

"We want the key," the man said.

Ramsey said nothing.

"Where is it?"

Ramsey said nothing.

The man slapped him again.

Rita cried out.

"Why don't you tell him, Matt?" Deputy Quinn, tied up in the adjoining chair, said to Ramsey.

Ramsey said, "You men are drunk, and in the morning you're really going to regret this."

This time the man raised a fist. It was obvious he was going to take pleasure in slugging Ramsey.

Deputy Quinn said, "Don't hit him, Earle. I'll tell you where the key is."

"Quinn!" Ramsey said. "Be quiet!"

"You know they'll kill you eventually, Matt. I don't want to see that happen."

"I don't want to see a lynching, either," Ramsey said.

"The keys are on the underside of the bottom drawer in this desk here."

Ramsey had feared the mood of the merchants, and so he'd hidden the keys earlier this evening while George Boyd had been here.

But they weren't hidden now.

Two merchants leaned over the desk, yanked out the bottom drawer and dangled the keys in Ramsey's face.

"Looks like luck is rolling our way now," one of the men said, and he grinned.

"Let's go get that son of a bitch," someone else said.

And suddenly the merchants were a mob again—mindless, angry, and eager.

Four men went to the cells at the back.

To the remaining merchants, Ramsey said, "Your town will never be the same after this."

"I guess that's for us to worry about."

Ramsey stared at the faces. Drunk, angry, hungry for some kind of excitement, the faces told Ramsey that right now these men were beyond any reason at all.

Ramsey glanced up at the clock.

An hour from now the train would be pulling in.

It would probably be too late for John Boyd, except as a funeral train.

When John Boyd heard the men coming, he pressed himself as far back against the bars of his cell as he could.

Then he frantically began searching for some kind of weapon, anything he could hold in his hands that would keep the men at bay.

But nothing was going to keep these men at bay.

They'd lived too long under the thumb of his father, and now his father was dead and they were going to extract the last bit of vengeance from the son.

The door leading to the cells was thrown open.

Four men came running back, one of them bearing a lantern that tossed warm yellow light over the damp, swollen walls.

Two of the men had carbines.

Earlier this evening, dozing off into a fitful sleep, John Boyd had had dreams about the hanging again. The one he'd seen as a young boy with his father.

Now the execution was going to be his.

Now the hooded hangman was going to be slipping the knot around his neck.

Outside, he could hear other men milling around, waiting for him to be brought to them.

Just like the hanging he'd witnessed as a young boy, there was going to be a crowd standing around tonight, one that would cheer on the events, one that would take great animal satisfaction in what it saw.

The men reached his cell.

"We're going to do you a favor, John," one of the men said.

"I just want you to leave me alone."

"We're not going to make you wait for that train. We're not going to put you through a trial."

"We're going to put an end to things right here," another man said.

"Just the way your father would have," the first man said.

This man fitted the key into the lock.

John could hear the lock turning, hear the cell door swinging back.

He had his eyes closed, his fists clenched.

This was all some terrible nightmare.

If only he could wake up and—

And in the nightmare he could see them now, the men, grabbing him roughly by the shirt and yanking him out of his cell.

Putting a gun muzzle to the back of his head and marching him toward the front of the jail.

"No, please," he said, and the sound of his own pleading sickened him.

But he did not want the hangman's knot slipping around his neck, did not want the horse slapped out from under him at the last minute, did not want the noose to snap his neck and leave him dangling.—

"No, please, please," he said again.

But they only pushed him harder toward the front of the jail.

Outside, the waiting men were starting to get even angrier. They craved excitement now; nothing less than a hanging was going to satisfy them.

"You want to go with us and watch it?" the merchant asked Matt Ramsey.

Ramsey just stared at him.

The man shrugged. "Just thought I'd be polite and ask. Some folks like to watch hangings."

The door leading to the cells was thrown back. John Boyd was pushed out into the office.

Dirty sweat glistened on his face. His blue eyes were wild with fear.

"Stop them, Sheriff. You've got to stop them," Boyd said.

He didn't seem to notice that Ramsey was tied and bound securely to the chair.

"I deserve a trial," Boyd said, looking pleadingly around at the men.

"Your father never gave this town a trial, son," one of the men said quietly. "For nearly twenty years he used us any way he wanted to."

"I'm not my father," Boyd said.

"No, but you're his son and you killed one of our girls and you deserve to hang for it."

"He also deserves a trial," Ramsey said.

The men in the dusty street outside had begun to call out for Boyd now. In the moonlit darkness, their voices rumbled with the hint of violence that was about to break wide open.

Rita said, "Please let him go."

Ramsey said. "The train'll be here in less than an hour."

Rita said, "It's not the right thing to do and you know it."

Boyd said, "For God's sake, listen to them, won't you?"

One of the merchants said, "The way your father used to listen to us, son?"

Another of the merchants said, "Maybe you don't know what it was like, boy, but any time your father wanted something from us, he just came into town here and took it. And there wasn't a damn thing we could do about it."

A rock came sailing through one of the front windows, quickly followed by another one.

Rita said, "Please, men. Please go tell them to go home and let the law take its course."

Two of the merchants got hold of young Boyd and pushed him toward the front door.

When the mob got its first look at Boyd, a cheer went up, as if they were all watching some kind of sporting event.

One of the merchants looked at Ramsey, his jaw set grimly, and said, "We'll be back soon enough, Sheriff."

Then he guided his prisoner outside to the waiting mob.

4

"You ever seen a hanging?" the bartender asked Thomas Peck.

Peck considered his drink a moment, as if the answer could be found in his shot glass. Then he shook his head. "Guess I haven't."

"I did. Just once. Never want to see another one, I can tell you that."

Peck was the man's only customer. Everybody else had become part of the lynch mob.

"He shit his pants."

Peck had been staring at his drink again, thinking. "Beg pardon?"

"He shit his pants."

"Who shit his pants?"

"The man they hanged."

"Oh."

"It was a real hot day and you could smell it."

"I see."

"And he didn't die like he was supposed to. Right away, I mean."

"He didn't?"

"No, it took a while. You could see him strangling and his eyes sort of pleading and all."

"They didn't use a hood?"

"No, this hanging took place over a Fourth of July weekend and they wanted everybody to have a real good time so they left the hood off."

"So how long did it take?"

"For him to die?"

"Yes."

"A good five minutes."

"That's a long time."

"He was wrenching every way imaginable. Kind of felt sorry for the son of a bitch, actually." He moved down to the end of the bar and looked out the window. All this time he held a small white towel, and he was wiping out this same glass again and again. "Wonder if they know how to do it."

"Hang him, you mean?"

The bartender nodded. "I don't hold much truck with the Boyds, of course, but then again I don't want to see the kid suffer, either."

Peck said, "Maybe I'll go watch."

He could see the disappointment in the bartender's face. Obviously the man didn't hold with lynching and thought he'd found a kindred spirit in Peck here, and obviously Peck had just proved him wrong.

"Going over there, huh?" the bartender asked.

"I've never seen a hanging."

"Not like you couldn't get through without seeing one." The bartender tried to sound wry. He just sounded bleak.

Thomas Peck downed his whiskey in a single gulp then rapped his knuckles on the bar.

"Be seeing you," he said, and he walked out into the night.

By now the crowd was reaching a kind of frenzy. He had to admit it was all frightening. Easy enough to imagine himself in Boyd's place, the hands tearing at you, pushing you toward the hanging tree . . .

He was going to watch the hanging, and then he was going to get his horse, and then he was going to ride fast and hard out of this town, and then he was never going to come back here again. Never.

He stepped down off the sidewalk and onto the dusty street.

They had torches now, the mob, and they were just now bringing Boyd to the big oak where they planned to hang him.

Thomas Peck felt his stomach start to knot up.
Then he moved toward the mob.

5

During the war, Ramsey had seen several lynchings, soldiers gone berserk with anger and grief, stringing up soldiers from the other side. Ramsey had never been there when the men were actually being hanged, but he'd seen them in the mornings, their faces blackened, their bodies torn apart by carrion birds.

Ramsey felt useless now, tied as he was to the chair, listening to the shouts of the merchants as they dragged John Boyd to the hanging tree.

Even with the cries of the mob, he could hear the protesting cries of John Boyd.

The poor bastard, Ramsey thought. Whatever his crime, he didn't deserve to end this way.

He deserved a court of law, and all the attendant rites; he didn't deserve to be dragged down a dusty street and lynched.

"They're going to do it, aren't they, Matt?" Rita Curry said. Like Deputy Quinn, Mort Boyd and Ramsey, she too was lashed to a chair.

"I'm afraid so."

"Not even my uncle George deserved this," Mort said.

"I'm sorry I told them where the key was," Deputy Quinn said.

"You didn't have any choice," Ramsey said.

And then they saw him.

Ramsey didn't know who he was, but the others seemed to recognize him.

GUNDOWN 155

A short man in a plaid drummer's suit too heavy for a hot night like this.

He walked right through the front door of the office, his fleshy face sweaty and curious at the sight of them.

"Evenin', Quinn," the man said.

"You going to untie us or you just going to stand there?" Quinn said.

"What the hell happened?"

Ramsey said, "Untie us first. We're in a hurry."

"There's a bowie knife in that desk drawer there," Quinn said. Then to Ramsey, "This is Fletcher. He's the night clerk at the hotel."

Fletcher was already at work.

He undid Rita first—he was a gentleman, apparently—and then he set to work on the others.

"They still lynchin' Boyd?" Fletcher asked as he worked.

"Unless we can stop them," Quinn said.

"Looks like they'll be lynchin' somebody else, too," Fletcher said, as he finished with Ramsey.

"What's that mean, Mr. Fletcher?" Ramsey said.

Fletcher shook his head. "That's why I came over here. Something happened at the hotel."

Ramsey stood up, rubbing his hands. "Deputy Quinn can help you. Right now I need to get over to the livery stable before they hang Boyd."

Ramsey walked over to the gun rack and took down a carbine. He started loading it immediately.

As soon as his own hands were free, Morty Boyd found his own gun and joined Ramsey as they headed out the door.

Somebody had started a fire in the hay next to the livery stable. The flames lit the night, a huge, roaring fire that painted yellow the men who stood around it.

From the broad oak tree on the other side of the livery dangled a hangman's knot.

In the flickering light of the flames, John Boyd was led to this tree, put on a horse and then had a black hood dropped over his head.

This was what Ramsey saw when he approached the mob, his carbine ready in his hands.

He fired two shots above the heads of the men, hoping that this would impress on them how serious he was about stopping the lynching.

At the sounds of the gunfire, the men stopped shouting, turned around and faced Ramsey and Mort Boyd.

"Get him down from that horse," Ramsey said. "And then you men go on home."

"This is our fight, not yours, Ramsey," a man said.

"You heard me," Ramsey said, moving closer to the mob.

He cocked the carbine, ready.

The horse Boyd sat on was still nervous from Ramsey's shots. The man standing next to it had to keep stroking it to keep it calm. The man looked disappointed that he hadn't yet been able to string the hangman's knot around Boyd's neck.

"Get him down from that horse," Ramsey said.

The men looked at each other. In the firelight, they appeared to be wearing grotesque ceremonial masks.

Ramsey started walking among the men now, toward the horse. If they wouldn't get Boyd down, then Ramsey would.

"Please help me, Sheriff," John Boyd said, sounding sick and a little crazed himself. "Please help me."

"Just stay calm," Ramsey said.

It was hot this close to the hay, and layers of golden heat were pouring over Ramsey's face now.

The light blinded him for a moment, and it was in that

moment that a man stepped out of the crowd and opened
fire.

Morty Boyd screamed. He was hit up high in the shoulder.

Ramsey's temporary blindness gave way to full vision
again. Ramsey saw the man—the haberdasher—lift his
Navy Colt and aim.

But Ramsey was ready.

He put two quick slugs into the man's chest.

The man went flailing backward, staggering in such a
way that he went directly toward the fire.

Before anyone could stop him, the haberdasher fell backward into the flames.

His screams were unrelenting on the night.

He lay in the center of the fire burning, burning.

Ramsey started toward the flaming man, to help pull him
from the flames. This left him vulnerable to attack, however, and so two merchants blindsided him, jumping him
and bringing two heavy weapons down hard across the back
of his head.

Ramsey pitched forward, feeling the carbine fall from his
hands, and lost consciousness.

"Smells awful, don't it?"

"Sure does."

"That's what made me curious."

"The smell?"

"The smell and the man in the room."

"What man?"

"Thomas Peck."

"What about him?"

Fletcher, the hotel clerk, shrugged as he led Deputy Quinn
up the stairs to the second floor. "Not sure. Just something

about him. You get to have a kind of second sense in this business."

"I suppose you do," Deputy Quinn said.

As they drew closer to the room, Deputy Quinn began to smell it, too. Something fetid. He'd once found a four-day-old corpse in a boating house. He'd never quite been able to forget the odor. This smell was something like that only not quite as pronounced.

Fletcher put the key into the door and let them in.

Deputy Quinn immediately clamped his hand over his nose.

The smell was much worse now.

Deputy Quinn looked around the room. There was some evidence of a recent brawl, a chair overturned, the bedclothes trailing on the floor.

But mostly it was the smell.

Down the street, the mob erupted again, its voice raucous and violent in the darkness. Deputy Quinn wanted to be with Ramsey but the lawman had insisted that the deputy come here.

Fletcher said, "Closet."

"Pardon?"

"The closet. That's where I bet it's coming from. The smell, I mean."

"You're probably right."

"You going to look in there?"

"Yes, I am."

"You mind if I *don't* look in there?"

"I guess not. Unless I need you to tell me who somebody is or something like that."

"I've got a queasy stomach. In general, I mean. And in particular around dead people. It's just the way I am."

Deputy Quinn nodded and walked over to the door.

Come to think of it, he had a queasy stomach where dead people were concerned, too. That's why his wife was always after him to get on over to the wagon works and give up law enforcement. A man shouldn't spend his working hours with criminals and dead people. It wasn't right.

Deputy Quinn took out his .45.

He walked up to the closet door.

The stench kept getting worse and worse.

Maybe a job over to the wagon works wouldn't be so bad after all.

He put a single gloved hand on the doorknob. Gave it a turn. The door opened.

Oh my God, he thought.

"If you don't mind, Deputy Quinn, I think I'll wait out in the hall."

"It's Sada from the whorehouse, and Robert Sayles," Deputy Quinn said.

He said this aloud because he felt he should say something, but he didn't know quite *what* to say.

"I'll be in the hall," Fletcher said.

Deputy Quinn backed away. He went over to the nightstand and picked up the kerosene lantern and got it lit and then he brought it back to the closet so he could get a better look at the two dead people.

Now that he thought about it, a job at the wagon works sounded better and better.

He closed the closet door, set down the kerosene lamp and went out into the hall.

"I've got to get over and talk to Matt," Deputy Quinn said to Fletcher, who still looked sick from the smell.

Fletcher nodded to the room. "I'll bet he killed Amanda Sayles, too, didn't he?"

Deputy Quinn nodded. "Don't let anybody go in there."

Fletcher surprised him by grinning. "You think anybody *wants* to get any closer to that smell?"

Deputy Quinn, who was not known for having the best sense of humor, simply shook his head. "I guess you're right there. It's pretty bad."

Then with that, he plunged down the stairs.

He had to get to Matt Ramsey. Fast.

6

Suddenly, everything went dark. He could hear their shouts and curses, he could feel the heat of the blazing fire, he could smell the shit that the horse beneath him kept dropping—but John Boyd couldn't see anything because they had dropped a black hood over his face.

And now they were cinching the hangman's knot around his neck.

The time had come.

By now he was so afraid he could no longer cry out, so afraid he couldn't stop his bowels from doing what they wanted, so afraid he couldn't stop the twitching that moved up and down his entire right side.

He tried to pray, but he found that he no longer believed in God. What sort of God would let this happen to him?

And then he heard the squeaking boots of the man in charge of his execution. They squeaked so loudly, he heard them even above the tumult, even above his own hammering heart.

Where was Ramsey now?

GUNDOWN   161

He'd heard gunshots earlier. Had they killed both Ramsey and Morty?

My God, he thought, he couldn't believe how these townsmen were acting. So crazy—

The boots came squeaking closer, closer.

Soon now the man would slap the backside of the horse and the horse would jerk away and John Boyd would—

Even now, even so late, even when it was obvious it was going to happen, he tried not to think about it.

The boots came squeaking closer, closer.

7

Thomas Peck liked the warmth of the blazing fire on his face and torso. There was something almost cheerful about it, how the huge fire lit the night, how the merchants—many of whom did not especially like each other—had bonded together here in a common purpose.

After they hanged John Boyd, Peck could go back to the hotel, quickly get his things and leave town.

By the time they found the two bodies, he'd be long gone, headed east toward a new life.

He looked at John Boyd now.

The man who'd stolen Amanda.

The man who'd caused him such grief.

Now John Boyd sat on a roan, a black hood over his head, the noose tight around his neck.

It wouldn't be long now before John Boyd would have to pay for all the grief he'd caused Thomas Peck.

It wouldn't be long now at all.

8

Matt Ramsey had been moved to the back of the mob, pushed up against a tree, his wrists bound.

From here he could see the back of the mob in stark silhouette, the flames of the fire burning in front of them, the hangman's rope angling down to the hooded man sitting the horse.

Ramsey had to wonder what this mob would do to him once it had temporarily sated its bloodlust on John Boyd. Mobs tended to be frenzied, hungry animals.

But all he could do now was sit, watch and squirm uselessly against his bonds.

Deputy Quinn ran down the center of the street toward the livery stable and the blooming flames.

Even from here, he could see the hangman's rope dangling down, and he wondered if he could turn back the mob in time.

And where was Matt? he wondered. What had they done with him?

He had reached the fringes of the mob when he heard his name called.

"Quinn!"

He stopped, chest heaving from his run, and looked around.

At first he saw nothing, his eyes night-blinded because of the fire.

"Quinn!"

Then through the murk, to his right and at the base of a tree, he saw the faint outline of a man.

Ramsey!

He hurried over there.

"Untie me," Ramsey said. "We've got to stop them!"

"Boyd isn't the killer, anyway. Thomas Peck is. And I'll bet he's in that mob right now."

He worked quickly on Ramsey's wrists, cutting them free in moments.

Ramsey said, struggling to his feet, "I'll need your carbine. They've got mine."

Deputy Quinn handed him the carbine. Then he drew his .45.

The mob paid them no attention. They were too interested in the spectacle that was about to take place.

"Hang him now!" somebody shouted.

And a great, abiding roar went up on the night.

Ramsey fired two shots in the air and waited for the mob to turn around.

"I'm ready to kill the first man who makes a move toward me," Ramsey said.

"John Boyd didn't murder Amanda Sayles," Deputy Quinn said. "Thomas Peck did."

"Thomas Peck!" somebody said. "Why, he's right here!"

But he wasn't.

Ramsey and Quinn searched the faces turned golden in the firelight, but neither could find Peck. He'd obviously taken off.

But the crowd would not be easily convinced.

"You're just saying that to stop us from hanging Boyd here!" somebody else said.

"If you hang him, you may hang an innocent man," Ramsey said.

He pushed through the crowd.

A burly man stepped forward to block his way.

Ramsey slammed the barrel of the carbine across the man's face. The man, spitting blood and crying out, fell to the ground, his jaw broken.

Ramsey moved the rest of the way to John Boyd without being interfered with.

He said to the merchant standing next to the horse, "Climb up in that tree and take that rope down."

"But he's the one who killed Amanda—"

Ramsey took his carbine and slammed the stock of it into the man's midsection, snapping a couple of ribs. As the man started to sink to his knees, Ramsey kicked the man in the chest, knocking him over backward.

"You," Ramsey said to another merchant, "you get up there and take that rope down."

"Yessir." This man was not about to give him any trouble.

Deputy Quinn came up. "One of us should go after Peck."

Ramsey smiled at him humorously. "I know. That's going to be my honor. You stay here and make sure that Boyd is all right."

Deputy Quinn nodded, trying not to make the pain from his arm so obvious by wincing. "Good luck, Matt."

Ramsey went up the back stairs of the hotel. From the different rooms came various smells—tobacco, whiskey, sweat.

He got on Peck's floor—having first looked at the book downstairs—and then moved silently down the hall.

Already, he was smelling the dead bodies.

Nothing else quite matched that gagging, sickening odor.

He could hear Peck inside there, obviously packing his bags.

Ramsey moved cautiously up to the door.

Eased it open with the barrel of the carbine.

Thomas Peck was bent over the bed, stuffing items into his large leather bag.

Ramsey said, "If you've got a gun, Mr. Peck, I'd advise you to set it down on the bed real easy."

Peck glanced over his shoulder. He tried to feign surprise. "Why are you bothering me, Sheriff. You've got your guilty man over by the livery stable."

"Care to show me what's in the closet?"

Peck sighed. "I don't know how they got there."

"I asked you about a firearm, Mr. Peck. If you've got one, put it down on the bed. That's the last time I'm going to tell you."

Peck made his move then, spinning away from the bed, ripping his gun from his holster, falling to one knee for a better shot.

Ramsey shot him three times in the chest.

Peck slammed backward against the bed, throwing his arms out as if he'd been crucified, then pitched face forward to the floor.

He was sobbing as he died.

The sound was lonely and horrible on the suddenly quiet air.

Ramsey went over to Peck, turned him over to look at his face.

He had, at most, moments to live.

Peck stared up at him with frightened brown eyes. "I loved her, Sheriff. I truly loved her."

And then he died.

Ramsey might have felt some pity for the man if the room didn't reek of two other people Peck had turned into corpses.

Peck hadn't shown them any mercy.

Ramsey wasn't about to show Peck any, either.

9

The train arrived on time.

Only one passenger boarded it: Matt Ramsey.

Rita and Deputy Quinn and Morty—who was heavily bandaged but going to be all right—stood on the platform as Ramsey boarded the train. Quinn had gotten some bandages, too.

Rita said, "We'd be glad to have you stay on as sheriff, Matt."

Ramsey nodded to Quinn. "There's the man for the job. I'm not ready to settle down just yet."

Morty Boyd said, "We owe you a lot, Matt."

Again, Ramsey nodded to Quinn. "There's the man who figured out who the real killer was. He should be wearing the badge, not me."

The conductor started shouting "Board! Board!" and the big steam engine sounded like a huge beast that just couldn't wait to go charging into the night.

"Thanks for helping Dad out," Rita Curry said, leaning forward and kissing Ramsey on the cheek.

On the other end of the platform stood the merchants. They were sober now, and disheveled, and looked like young boys ashamed of something they'd done.

"It's your town now, Deputy Quinn," Ramsey said, tossing him the star that Sam Curry had worn so proudly. "Take good care of it."

And then he was on the train, Matt Ramsey, headed into the night and whatever awaited him down the line.

An American Family   An American Dream

THE RAMSEYS

Will McLennan

Bound to the land and united by their blood, the Ramseys have survived for generations. Brave, sturdy, and strong-willed, they have forged out a rugged new life in North Texas, overcoming drought, disease, and the mayhem of the Civil War. Every Ramsey is born to fight for justice and freedom on the American Frontier.

__ #1	THE RAMSEYS	0-515-10009-9/$2.95
__ #2	RAMSEY'S LUCK	0-515-10129-X/$2.95
__ #4	BLOOD MONEY	0-515-10214-8/$2.95
__ #5	RAMSEY'S GOLD	0-515-10269-5/$2.95
__ #6	DEATH TRAIL	0-515-10307-1/$2.95
__ #7	RAMSEY'S BADGE	0-515-10350-0/$2.95
__ #8	THE DEADLY STRANGER	0-515-10400-0/$2.95
__ #9	COMANCHE	0-515-10444-2/$2.95
__ #10	BAD BLOOD	0-515-10493-0/$2.95
__ #11	DEATH HUNT	0-515-10525-2/$2.95

For Visa, MasterCard and American Express orders call: 1-800-631-8571

FOR MAIL ORDERS: CHECK BOOK(S). FILL OUT COUPON. SEND TO:

BERKLEY PUBLISHING GROUP
390 Murray Hill Pkwy., Dept. B
East Rutherford, NJ 07073

NAME_____
ADDRESS_____
CITY_____
STATE_____ ZIP_____

PLEASE ALLOW 6 WEEKS FOR DELIVERY.
PRICES ARE SUBJECT TO CHANGE WITHOUT NOTICE.

POSTAGE AND HANDLING:
$1.00 for one book, 25¢ for each additional. Do not exceed $3.50.

BOOK TOTAL $ ____
POSTAGE & HANDLING $ ____
APPLICABLE SALES TAX $ ____
(CA, NJ, NY, PA)
TOTAL AMOUNT DUE $ ____
PAYABLE IN US FUNDS.
(No cash orders accepted.)

327

A special offer for people who enjoy reading the best Westerns published today. If you enjoyed this book, subscribe now and get...

TWO FREE

A $5.90 VALUE—NO OBLIGATION

If you enjoyed this book and would like to read more of the very best Westerns being published today, you'll want to subscribe to True Value's Western Home Subscription Service. If you enjoyed the book you just read and want more of the most exciting, adventurous, action packed Westerns, subscribe now.

Each month the editors of True Value will select the 6 very best Westerns from America's leading publishers for special readers like you. You'll be able to preview these new titles as soon as they are published, FREE for ten days with no obligation.

TWO FREE BOOKS

When you subscribe, we'll send you your first month's shipment of the newest and best 6 Westerns for you to preview. With your first shipment, two of these books will be yours as our introductory gift to you absolutely FREE, regardless of what you decide to do. If you like them, as much as we think you will, keep all six books but pay for just 4 at the low subscriber rate of just $2.45 each. If you decide to return them, keep 2 of the titles as our gift. No obligation.

Special Subscriber Savings

When you become a True Value subscriber you'll save money several ways. First, all regular monthly selections will be billed at the low subscriber price of just $2.45 each. That's